ALAIN ROBBE-GRILLET was born in Bres͏ͅ ͏ͅer obtaining a degree as an agron͏ͅ ͏ͅneer, he worked at the National Insti͏ͅu͏ͅ for Statistics in Paris, before undertaking field work for the Institute of Colonial Fruit and Citrus Fruit in Morocco, Guinea, Martinique and Guadeloupe. His first novel *Les Gommes* (*The Erasers*) was published in 1953 and heralded a new type of fiction which favoured perception, description and imagination over plot and characterization. From the 1960s onwards he became a prolific avant-garde scriptwriter and film director. His fiercely independent and rebellious stance led to clashes and controversies with the establishment, with Robbe-Grillet famously rejecting election into the prestigious Académie Française. He died in Caen in 2008.

ALMA CLASSICS LTD
London House
243-253 Lower Mortlake Road
Richmond
Surrey TW9 2LL
United Kingdom
www.almaclassics.com

First published in French as *La Jalousie* in 1957 by Les Éditions de Minuit, Paris
© Les Editions Minuit, 1957
Translation © Grove Press, New York, 1959
First published in Great Britain in 1960 by John Calder Limited
This edition first published by Alma Classics Limited in 2008
Introduction © Tom McCarthy, 2008

Printed and bound by CPI Group (UK) Ltd, Croydon, CR0 4YY

ISBN: 978-1-84749-272-2

Jealousy

Alain Robbe-Grillet

Translated by Richard Howard

With an Introduction by Tom McCarthy

ALMA CLASSICS

Introduction

The Geometry of the Pressant

Alain Robbe-Grillet died while I was writing this introduction. The obituaries he received in the British press depicted him as a significant but ultimately eccentric novelist whose work forswore any attempt to be "believable" or to engage with the real world in a "realistic" way. In taking this line, the obituarists displayed an intellectual shortcoming typical of Anglo-American empiricism, and displayed it on two fronts: firstly, in their failure to understand that literary "realism" is itself a construct as laden with artifice as any other; and secondly, in missing the glaring fact that Robbe-Grillet's novels are actually ultra-realist, shot through at every level with the sheer *quiddity* of the environments to which they attend so faithfully. What we see happening in them, again and again, is space and matter inscribing themselves on consciousness, whose task, reciprocally, is to accommodate space and matter. As Robbe-Grillet was himself fond of declaring: "No art without world".

This type of intense congress with the real can be seen even in Robbe-Grillet's shortest offerings. In the three-page story 'The Dressmaker's Dummy' (which opens the collection *Snapshots*), we are shown a coffee pot, a four-legged table, a waxed tablecloth, a mannequin and, crucially, a large rectangular mirror that reflects the room's objects – which include a mirror-fronted wardrobe that in turn redoubles everything. Thus we are made to navigate a set of duplications, modifications and distortions that are at once almost impossibly complex and utterly accurate: this is how rooms actually look to an observer, how their angles, surfaces and sight lines impose themselves on his or her perception. No other action takes place in the piece, which nonetheless ends with a quite stunning "twist" as we are told that the coffee pot's base bears a picture of an owl "with two large, somewhat frightening eyes" but, due to the coffee pot's presence, this image cannot be seen. What waits for us at the story's climax, its gaze directed back towards our own, is a blind spot.

In *Jealousy*, this blind spot is the novel's protagonist. Through a meticulously – indeed, obsessively – described house, set in the middle of a tropical banana plantation, moves what film-makers call a POV or "point of view": a camera and mic-like "node" of seeing and hearing. The one thing not seen or heard by this node is the node itself. Phrases such as "it takes a glance at her empty though stained plate to discover…" and "Memory succeeds, moreover, in reconstituting…" beg the questions: whose glance? whose memory? The answer, it can pretty easily be inferred from the novel's context, is that it is the master of the house's glance and memory, his movements and reflections we are experiencing as he watches his wife, identified only as "A…", negotiate an affair with the neighbouring plantation owner, Franck. The effect of stating the hero's subjectivity negatively, by implication rather than affirmation, is eerie and troubling: his gaze becomes like that of "The Shape" in John Carpenter's *Halloween*, or the entity in David Lynch's *Lost Highway* who stalks a maritally troubled house at night armed with a camera. When we read that "it is only at a distance of less than a yard" that the back of A…'s head appears a certain way, we realize with a shudder that her jealous husband is creeping up on her from behind. He is observing her, in this particular instance, through the slats of a blind (or *jalousie* in French); and we, through an ingenious if untranslatable linguistic duplication, are watching her through two *jalousies*: a double blind.

The novel is saturated with a sense of geometry. The house's surfaces reveal themselves to us in a series of straight lines and chevrons, horizontals, verticals and diagonals, discs and trapezoids. The banana trees, as green as jealousy itself, are laid out in quincunxes, as are the workers who replace the bridge's rectangular beams. Geometric order is pitted against formlessness and entropy: on the far side of the valley, towards Franck's house, is a patch in which the narrator tells us, using language reminiscent of Othello's, that "confusion has gained the ascendancy". As A... combs her hair, the struggle between geometry and chaos is replayed: with a "mechanical gesture" the oval of the brush and straight lines of its teeth pass through the "black mass" on her head, imposing order on it, just as the "mechanical cries" of nocturnal animals shape the darkness beyond the veranda by indicating each one's "trajectory through the night". Geometry usually wins: even the "tangled skein" of insects buzzing round the lamp reveal themselves, when observed at length by the husband, to be "describing more or less flattened ellipses in horizontal planes or at slight angles". But an ellipse is not merely a type of orbit; it also designates a syntactical omission, a typographic gap. What's missing from this geometry is A..., the character whose very name contains an ellipse: during this particular scene she is off in town with Franck. As the narrator waits for her to come home, the lamp hisses, like a green-eyed monster.

Enmeshed with the book's spatial logic is a temporal one. The second time we see the shadow of the column fall on the veranda it has lengthened in a clockwise direction, the geometry of the house effectively forming a sundial. In a filmed interview with curator Hans Ulrich Obrist (Robbe-Grillet's influence on contemporary visual art is enormous), Robbe-Grillet ponders Hegel's paradox that to say "Now it is day" cannot be wholly true if, a few hours later, one can equally truthfully declare "Now it is night", and notes that, for Hegel, the only true part of both statements is the word "now". Why? Because it persists. The same word punctuates *Jealousy* like the regular chime of a clock: "Now the shadow of the column..."; "Now the house is empty..."; "...until the day breaks, now".

This is not to say that time moves forwards in a straight line. Like Benjy in William Faulkner's *The Sound and the Fury*, *Jealousy*'s narrator experiences time – or times – simultaneously. For Robbe-Grillet, who also made films, writing is like splicing strips of celluloid together to create a continual present. There are prolepses, analepses, loops and repetitions (a process slyly

...rrored in the staggering of the plantation cycle through the whole year such that all its phases "occur at the same time every day, and the periodical trivial incidents also repeat themselves simultaneously"), but the time is always "now". A delightful exchange between the husband and the serving boy, in which the latter answers a question as to when he was instructed to retrieve ice cubes from the pantry with an imprecise "now" (discerning in the question "a request to hurry"), carries this point home: all the book's actions and exchanges swelter in a stultifying, oppressive and persistent present tense – what Joyce, in *Finnegans Wake*, calls "the pressant".

The only escape route from this "pressant", from its simultaneity, its loops and repetitions, would be violence: for the narrator to perpetrate a *crime passionnel* against A... and, by murdering her, free them from the vicious circle of meals, cocktails, hair-combing, spying. But this does not happen. Only the centipede dies: again and again and again. The venomous *Scutigera* serves as a meeting point for associations so overloaded that if it were a plug socket it would be smoking. During one of its many death scenes, the narrative cuts from the crackling of its dying scream as its many legs curl to the crackling sound made by the many teeth of A...'s brush running through her hair; then on to A...'s fingers clenching the tablecloth in terror; from there to the same gesture played out across the bedsheet; then finally to Franck "jolting" and "driving" violently – a sexual image that resolves itself into a putative crash in which Franck's burning car makes the bush crackle. As with Franck's car crash, posited and then erased, it seems that A... has finally met a violent fate when, near the novel's end, we are shown a "reddish streak" running from the bedroom window to the veranda. But no sooner is it outlined than we are told that it "has always been there", and that A... has decided it will not be painted out "for the moment". So the moment, the eternal "now", persists, and she returns to sit at her desk as before.

A... is a fantastic creation, a femme fatale to rival Lady Macbeth or Clytemnestra in terms of her castrating potency. Throughout the book, Robbe-Grillet associates her with the colour green ("green eyes... green irises") and coldness: she serves ice cubes "each of which imprisons a bundle of silver needles in its heart". A twist rears its head when, after she and Franck return from their night in a hotel, she taunts Franck (whose sexuality has been associated with car engines from the outset) by saying: "you're not much of a mechanic, are you?" – words that cause him to grimace. Later, as they sit side by side, our attention is diverted to the metal ice bucket, "its lustre already frosted over". If A... retreats from the narrator, she retreats from Franck as well, remaining inaccessible to both. Perhaps the literary female she resembles most is another A...: Faulkner's Addie Bundren in *As I Lay Dying*, who, despite marriage and an extra-marital affair, abides "refraining" and "recessional" beyond the reach of both husband and lover, and of words themselves. As *Jealousy* nears its end, A..., like Addie, slips away into the "blank areas" of the book's geometry, spending more and more time "outside the field of vision", as though commandeering the narrator's blind spot for herself.

One of A...'s main activities throughout the novel is to read and write. She and Franck use a novel, which they have both read and the narrator has not, as a cover to discuss their own situation right in front of him. They also exchange letters. The small spasms and convulsions of A...'s hair as she sits at her writing table, busy hands hidden from view, lend the act of writing a sexual aura by implying that she could as easily be masturbating as "erasing a stain or a badly chosen word". In this respect, there is something utterly perverse – doubly perverse – about her husband's perusal of her writing's residues, the fragments of letters left on the writing case's blotter. These, too, are geometric figures: "tiny lines, arcs, crosses, loops, etc." – but, unlike the centipede whose form is marked so legibly across the wall (before being erased and reinscribed, over and over again), here "no complete letter can be made out, even in a mirror"; the text remains illegible.

In the same interview with Obrist, Robbe-Grillet claims that, whereas the novels of Balzac or Dickens do not require readers, since they perform all the latter's work themselves, his own writing calls for active readers who will piece it all together. It is like an Airfix kit – but there is always one vital piece missing. The final letter we see A… reading has come not from Franck but rather in "the last post from Europe", from an unknown correspondent. As she sets a blank leaf on her green blotter, removes her pen's cap and bends forwards to start writing, one more twist emerges: within the self-reflexive geometries of Robbe-Grillet's hall of mirrors, the ultimate blind spot might just be the reader.

– Tom McCarthy, 2008

Jealousy

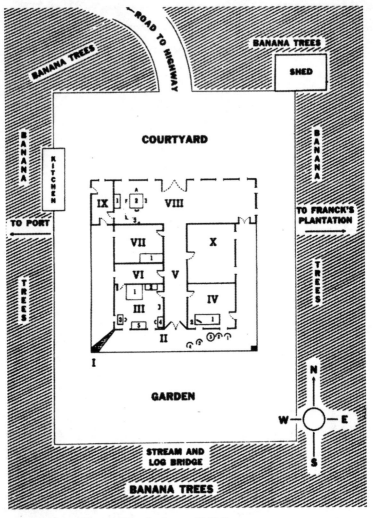

I. **South-west pillar and its shadow at the beginning of the novel**

II. **Veranda:** 1) Franck's chair; 2) A...'s chair; 3) Empty chair; 4) Husband's chair; 5) Coffee table

III. **A...'s room:** 1) Bed; 2) Chest; 3) Dressing table; 4) Writing table; 5) Wardrobe

IV. **Office:** 1) Desk; 2) Photo of A...

V. **Hallway**

VI. **Bathroom**

VII. **Small bedroom:** 1) Bed

VIII. **Living room /dining room:** 1) Buffet; 2) Table; 3) Centipede mark on wall

IX. **Pantry**

X. **Storage room or other (not described)**

N OW THE SHADOW of the column – the column which supports the south-west corner of the roof – divides the corresponding corner of the veranda into two equal parts. This veranda is a wide, covered gallery surrounding the house on three sides. Since its width is the same for the central portion as for the sides, the line of shadow cast by the column extends precisely to the corner of the house – but it stops there, for only the veranda flagstones are reached by the sun, which is still too high in the sky. The wooden walls of the house – that is, its front and west gable end – are still protected from the sun by the roof (common to the house proper and the terrace). So at this moment the shadow of the outer edge of the roof coincides exactly with the right angle formed by the terrace and the two vertical surfaces of the corner of the house.

Now A... has come into the bedroom by the inside door opening onto the central hallway. She does not look at the wide-open window through which – from the door – she would see this corner of the terrace. Now she has turned back towards the door to close it behind her. She still has on the light-coloured, close-fitting dress with the high collar that she was wearing at lunch when Christiane reminded her again that loose-fitting clothes make the heat easier to bear. But A... merely smiled: she never suffered from the heat, she had known much worse climates than this – in Africa, for instance – and had always felt fine there. Besides, she doesn't feel the cold either. Wherever she is, she keeps quite comfortable. The black curls of her hair shift with a supple movement and brush her shoulders as she turns her head.

The heavy handrail of the balustrade has almost no paint left on top. The grey of the wood shows through, streaked with longitudinal cracks. On the other side of this rail, a good six feet below the level of the veranda, the garden begins.

But from the far side of the bedroom the eye carries over the balustrade and only touches ground much further away, on the opposite slope of the little valley, among the banana trees of the plantation. The sun cannot be seen between their thick clusters of wide green leaves. However, since this sector has been under cultivation only recently, the regular criss-crossing of the rows of trees can still be clearly followed. The same is true of almost all the property visible from here, for the older sectors – where confusion has gained the ascendancy – are located higher up on this side of the valley – that is, on the other side of the house.

It is on the other side, too, that the highway passes, just below the edge of the plateau. This highway, the only road that gives access to the property, marks its northern border. A dirt road leads from the highway to the sheds and, lower still, to the house, in front of which a large cleared area with a very slight slope permits cars to be turned around.

The house is built on a level with this courtyard, from which it is separated by no veranda or gallery. On the three other sides, however, it is enclosed by the veranda.

The slope of the terrain, more pronounced from the start of the courtyard, causes the central portion of the veranda (which runs along the front of the house on the south) to stand at least six feet above the garden.

On all sides of the garden, as far as the borders of the plantation, stretches the green mass of the banana trees.

On the right and the left, their proximity is too great, combined with the veranda's relative lack of elevation, to permit an observer stationed there to distinguish the arrangement of the trees – while further down the valley, the quincunx can be made out at first glance. In certain very recently replanted sectors – those where the reddish earth is just beginning to yield supremacy to foliage – it is easy enough to follow the regular perspective of the four intersecting lanes along which the young trunks are aligned.

This exercise is not much more difficult, despite their more advanced growth, for those sectors of the plantations on the opposite hillside: this, in fact, is the place which offers itself most readily to inspection, the place over which surveillance can be maintained with the least difficulty (although the path to reach it is a long one), the place which the eye falls on quite naturally of its own accord, when looking out of one or the other of the two open windows of the bedroom.

Her back to the hall door she has just closed, A... absently stares at the paint-flaked wood of the balustrade, nearer her the paint-flaked window frame, then, nearer still, the scrubbed wood of the door.

She takes a few steps into the room, goes over to the heavy chest and opens its top drawer. She shifts the papers in the right-hand side of the drawer, leans over and, in order to see the rear of the drawer better, pulls it a little further out of the chest. After looking a little longer, she straightens up and remains motionless, elbows close to her body, forearms bent and hidden by the upper part of her body – probably holding a sheet of paper between her hands.

She turns towards the light now in order to continue reading without straining her eyes. Her inclined profile does not move any more. The paper is pale-blue, the size of ordinary letter paper, and shows the creases where it had been folded into quarters.

Then, holding the letter in one hand, A... closes the drawer, moves towards the little work table (near the second window, against the partition separating the bedroom from the hallway) and sits down in front of the writing case, from which she removes a sheet of pale-blue paper – similar to the first, but blank. She unscrews the cap of her pen, then, after a glance to the right (which does not include even the middle of the window frame behind her), bends her head towards the writing case in order to begin writing.

The lustrous black hair falls in motionless curls along the line of her back, which the narrow metal fastening of her dress indicates a little lower down.

Now the shadow of the column – the column which supports the south-west corner of the roof – lengthens across the flagstones of the central part of the veranda, in front of the house where the chairs have been set out for the evening. Already the tip of the line of shadow almost touches the doorway which marks the centre of the façade. Against the west gable end of the house, the sun falls on the wood about a yard and a half above the flagstone. Through the third window, which looks out on this side, it would reach far into the bedroom if the blinds had not been lowered.

The pantry is at the other end of this west wing of the veranda. Through its half-open door A...'s voice can be heard, then that of the black cook, voluble and sing-song, then again the clear, moderate voice, giving orders for the evening meal.

The sun has disappeared behind the rocky spur that ends the main section of the plateau.

Sitting facing the valley, in one of the armchairs of local manufacture, A... is reading the novel borrowed the day before; they have already spoken about it at noon. She continues reading, without raising her eyes, until the daylight becomes too faint. Then she raises her head, closes the book – which she puts within arm's reach on the coffee table – and remains staring straight in front of her, towards the openwork balustrade and the banana trees on the opposite slope, that are soon invisible in the darkness. She seems to be listening to the noise that rises on all sides from the thousands of crickets inhabiting the low ground. But it is a continuous, ear-splitting sound without variations, in which nothing can be distinguished.

Franck is here again for dinner, smiling, talkative, affable. Christiane has not come with him this time; she has stayed home with the child, who is running a slight fever. It is not unusual, these days, for the husband to come without her like this, because of the child, because of Christiane's own ailments – for her health has difficulty adapting itself to this hot, humid climate – and also because of her domestic problems, her difficulties managing her too numerous and poorly organized servants.

Tonight, though, A... seemed to expect her. At least she had had four places set. She gives orders to have the one that will not be used taken away at once.

On the veranda, Franck drops into one of the low armchairs and utters his usual exclamation as to how comfortable they are. They are very simple chairs of wood and leather thongs, made according to A...'s instructions by a native craftsman. She leans towards Franck to hand him his glass.

Although it is quite dark now, she has given orders that the lamps should not be brought out, because – she says – they attract mosquitoes. The glasses are filled almost to the brim with a mixture of cognac and soda in which a little cube of ice is floating. In order to avoid the danger of upsetting the glasses in the darkness, A... has moved as near as possible to the armchair Franck is sitting in, her right hand carefully extending the glass with his drink in it. She rests her other hand on the arm of the chair and bends over him, so close that their heads touch. He murmurs a few words: probably thanking her.

She straightens up gracefully, picks up the third glass – which she is not afraid of spilling, for it is much less full – and sits down besides Franck, while he continues telling the story about his engine trouble that he had begun the moment he arrived.

It was A... who arranged the chairs this evening, when she had them brought out on the veranda. The one she invited Franck to sit in and her own are side by side against the wall of the house – backs against this wall, of course – beneath the office window. So that Franck's chair is on her left, and on her right – but further forwards – the little table where the bottles are. The two other chairs are placed on the other side of this table, still further to the right, so that they do not block the view of the first two through the balustrade of the veranda. For the same reason these last two chairs are not turned to face the rest of the group: they have been set at an angle, obliquely orientated towards the openwork balustrade and the hillside opposite. This arrangement obliges anyone sitting there to turn his head around sharply towards the left if he wants to see A... – especially anyone in the fourth chair, which the furthest away.

The third, which is a folding chair made of canvas stretched on a metal frame, occupies a distinctly retired position between the fourth chair and the table. But it is this chair, less comfortable, which has remained empty.

Franck's voice continues describing the day's problems on his own plantation. A... seems to be interested in them. She encourages him from time to time by a few words indicating her attention. During a pause the sound of a glass being put down on the little table can be heard.

On the other side of the balustrade, towards the opposite hillside, there is only the sound of the crickets and starless dark of the night. In the dining room the two kerosene lamps are lit. One is at the edge of the long sideboard, towards its left end; the other on the table itself, in the empty place of the fourth guest.

The table is square, since extra leaves (unnecessary for so few people) have not been added. The three places set are on three sides, the lamp on the fourth. A... is at her usual place; Franck is sitting at her right – therefore with his back to the sideboard.

On the sideboard, to the left of the second lamp (that is, on the side of the open pantry door), are piled the clean plates which will be used during the meal. To the right of the lamp and behind it – against the wall – a native terracotta pitcher marks the middle of the sideboard. Further to the right, against the grey-painted wall, is outlined the magnified and blurred shadow of a man's head – Franck's. He is wearing neither jacket nor tie, and the collar of his shirt is unbuttoned, but the shirt itself is irreproachably white, made of a thin material of high quality, the French cuffs held together by detachable ivory links.

A... is wearing the same dress she wore at lunch. Franck almost had an argument with his wife about it, when Christiane criticized its cut as being "too hot for this country". A... merely smiled: "Besides, I don't find the climate here so bad as all that," she said, to change the subject. "If you could imagine how hot it was ten months out of the year in Kanda!..." Then the conversation had settled for a while on Africa.

The boy comes in through the open pantry door, holding the tureen full of soup in both hands. As soon as he puts it down, A... asks him to move the lamp on the table, whose glare – she says – hurts her eyes. The boy lifts the lamp by the handle and carries it to the other end of the room, setting it down on a piece of furniture A... points to with her left hand.

The table is immediately plunged into shadow. Its chief source of light has become the lamp on the sideboard, for the second lamp – in the opposite direction – is now much further away.

On the wall, towards the pantry door, Franck's head has disappeared. His white shirt no longer gleams as it did just now beneath the direct light of the lamp on the table. Only his right sleeve is reached by the beams of the lamp three quarters of the way behind him: the shoulder and the arm are edged with a bright line and, similarly, higher up, the ear and neck. His face has the light almost directly behind it.

"Don't you think that's better?" A... asks, turning towards him.

"Certainly more intimate," Franck answers.

He drinks his soup in rapid spoonfuls. Although he makes no excessive gestures, although he holds his spoon quite properly and swallows the liquid without making any noise, he seems to display, in this modest task, a disproportionate level of energy and zest. It would be difficult to specify exactly in what way he is neglecting some essential rule, at what particular point he is lacking in discretion.

Avoiding any notable defect, his behaviour nevertheless does not pass unnoticed. And, by contrast, it accentuates the fact that A... has just completed the same operation without having seemed to move – but without attracting any attention, on the other hand, by an abnormal immobility. It takes a glance at her empty though stained plate to discover that she has not neglected to serve herself.

Memory succeeds, moreover, in reconstituting several movements of her right hand and her lips, several comings and goings of the spoon between the plate and her mouth, which might be considered as significant.

To be still more certain, it is enough to ask her if she doesn't think the cook has made the soup too salty.

"Oh no," she answers, "you have to eat salt so as not to sweat."

Which, on reflection, does not prove beyond a doubt that she tasted the soup today.

Now the boy clears away the plates. It then becomes impossible to check again the stains on A...'s plate – or their absence, if she has not served herself.

The conversation has returned to the story of the engine trouble: in the future Franck will not buy any more old military equipment; his latest acquisitions have given him too many problems; the next time he replaces one of his vehicles, it will be with a new one.

But he is wrong to trust modern trucks to the black drivers, who will wreck them just as fast, if not faster.

"All the same,' Franck says, "if the motor is new, the driver will not have to fool with it.'

Yet he should know that just the opposite is true: the new motor will be all the more attractive a toy, and what with speeding on bad roads and acrobatics behind the wheel…

On the strength of his three years' experience, Franck believes there are good drivers even among the black people here. A… is also of this opinion, of course.

She has kept out of the discussion about the comparative quality of the machines, but the question of the drivers provokes a rather long and categorical intervention on her part.

Besides, she might be right. In that case, Franck would have to be right too.

Both are now talking about the novel A… is reading, whose action takes place in Africa. The heroine cannot bear the tropical climate (like Christiane). The heat actually seems to give her terrible attacks:

"It's all in the mind, things like that," Franck says.

He then makes a reference, obscure for anyone who has not even leafed through the book, to the husband's behaviour. His sentence ends with "take apart" or "take a part", without it being possible to be sure who or what is meant. Franck looks at A…, who is looking at Franck. She gives him a quick smile that is quickly absorbed in the shadows. She has understood, since she knows the story.

No, her features have not moved. Their immobility is not so recent: the lips have remained set since her last words. The fugitive smile must have been a reflection of the lamp, or the shadow of a moth.

Besides, she was no longer facing Franck at that moment. She had just moved her head back and was looking straight ahead of her down the table, towards the bare wall where a blackish spot marks the place where a centipede was squashed last week, at the beginning of the month, perhaps the month before, or later.

Franck's face, with the light almost directly behind it, does not reveal the slightest expression.

The boy comes in to clear away the plates. A... asks him, as usual, to serve the coffee on the veranda.

Here the darkness is complete. No one talks any more. The sound of the crickets has stopped. Only the shrill cry of some nocturnal carnivore can be heard from time to time, and the sudden drone of a beetle, the clink of a little porcelain cup being set on the coffee table.

Franck and A... have sat down in their same two chairs, backs against the wooden wall of the house. It is once again the chair with the metal frame which has remained unoccupied. The position of the fourth chair is still less justified, now that there is no view over the valley. (Even before dinner, during the brief twilight, the apertures of the balustrade were too narrow to permit a real view of the landscape, and above the handrail nothing but sky could be seen.)

The wood of the balustrade is smooth to the touch, when the fingers follow the direction of the grain and the tiny longitudinal cracks. A scaly zone comes next; then there is another smooth surface, but this time without lines of orientation and stippled here and there with slight rough-nesses in the paint.

In broad daylight, the contrast of the two shades of grey – that of the naked wood and that, somewhat lighter, of the remaining paint – creates complicated figures with angular, almost serrated outlines. On the top of the handrail, there are only scattered, protruding islands formed by the last vestiges of paint. On the balusters, though, it is the unpainted areas, much smaller and generally located towards the middle of the uprights, which constitute the spots, here incised, where the fingers recognize the vertical grain of the wood. At the edge of the patches, new scales of the paint are easy to chip off; it is enough to slip a fingernail beneath the projecting edge and pry it up by bending the first joint of the finger; the resistance is scarcely perceptible.

On the other side of the veranda, once the eye is accustomed to the darkness, a paler form can be seen outlined against the wall of the house: Franck's white shirt. His forearms are lying on the elbow rests. The upper part of his body is leaning back in the chair.

A... is humming a dance tune whose words remain unintelligible. But perhaps Franck understands them, if he already knows them, from having heard them often, perhaps with her. Perhaps it is one of her favourite records.

A...'s arms, a little less distinct than her neighbour's because of the colour – though light – of the material of her dress, are also lying on the elbow rests of her chair. The four hands are lying in a row, motionless. The space between A...'s left hand and Franck's right hand is approximately two inches. The shrill cry of some nocturnal carnivore, sharp and short, echoes again towards the bottom of the valley, at an unspecifiable distance.

"I think I'll be getting along," Franck says.

"Oh don't go," A... replied at once, "it's not late at all. It's so pleasant sitting out here."

If Franck wanted to leave, he would have a good excuse: his wife and child who are alone in the house. But he mentions only the hour he must get up the next morning, without making any reference to Christiane. The same shrill, short cry, which sounds closer, now seems to come from the garden, quite near the foot of the veranda on the east side.

As if echoing it, a similar cry follows, coming from the opposite direction. Others answer these, from higher up, towards the road, then still others, from the low ground.

Sometimes the sound is a little lower, or more prolonged. There are probably different kinds of animals. Still, all these cries are alike; not that their common characteristic is easy to decide, but rather their common lack of characteristics: they do not seem to be cried out of fright, or pain, or intimidation, or even love. They sound like mechanical cries, uttered without perceptible motive, expressing nothing, indicating only the existence, the position and the respective movements of each animal, whose trajectory through the night they punctuate.

"All the same," Franck says, "I think I'll be getting along."

A... does not reply. Neither one has moved. They are sitting side by side, leaning back in their chairs, arms lying on the elbow rests, their four hands in similar positions, at the same level, lined up parallel to the wall of the house.

Now the shadow of the south-west column – at the corner of the veranda on the bedroom side – falls across the garden. The sun, still low in the eastern sky, rakes the valley from the side. The rows of banana trees, growing at an angle to the direction of the valley, are everywhere quite distinct in this light.

From the bottom to the upper edge of the highest sectors, on the hillside facing the one the house is built on, it is relatively easy to count the trees – particularly opposite the house, thanks to the recent plantings of the patches located in this area.

The valley has been cleared over the greater part of its width here: there remains, at present, nothing but a border of brush (some thirty yards across at the top of the plateau) which joins the valley by a knoll with neither crest nor rocky fall.

The line of separation between the uncultivated zone and the banana plantation is not entirely straight. It is a zigzag line, with alternately protruding and receding angles, each belonging to a different patch of different age, but of a generally identical orientation.

Just opposite the house, a clump of trees marks the highest point the cultivation reaches in this sector. The patch that ends here is a rectangle. The ground is invisible, or virtually so, between the fronds. Still, the impeccable alignment of the boles shows that they have been planted only recently and that no stems have as yet been cut.

Starting from this clump of trees, the patch runs downhill with a slight divergence (towards the left) from the greatest angle of slope. There are thirty-two banana trees in the row, down to the lower edge of the patch.

Prolonging this patch towards the bottom, with the same arrangement of rows, another patch occupies the space between the first patch and the little stream that flows through the valley bottom. This second patch is twenty-three trees deep, and only its more advanced vegetation distinguishes it from the preceding patch: the greater height of the trunks, the tangle of fronds and the number of well-formed stems. Besides, some stems have already been cut. But the empty place where the bole has been cut is then as easily discernible as the tree itself would be, with its tuft of wide, pale-green leaves, out of which comes the thick curving stem bearing the fruit.

Furthermore, instead of being rectangular like the one above it, this patch is trapezoidal; for the stream bank that constitutes its lower edge is not perpendicular to its two sides – running up the slope – which are parallel to each other. The row on the right side has no more than thirteen banana trees instead of twenty-tree.

And finally, the lower edge of this patch is not straight, since the little stream is not: a slight bulge narrows the patch towards the middle of its width. The central row, which should have eighteen trees if it were to be a true trapezoid, has, in fact, only sixteen.

In the second row, starting from the far left, there would be twenty-two trees (because of the alternate arrangement) in the case of a rectangular patch. There would also be twenty-two for a patch that was precisely trapezoidal, the reduction being scarcely noticeable at such a short distance from its base. And, in fact, there are twenty-two trees there.

But the third row too has only twenty-two trees, instead of twenty-three, which the alternately arranged rectangle would have. No additional difference is introduced, at this level, by the bulge in the lower edge. The same is true for the fourth row, which includes twenty-two boles – that is, one less than an even row of the imaginary rectangle.

The bulge of the bank also begins to take effect starting from the fifth row: this row, as a matter of fact, also possesses only twenty-one trees, whereas it should have twenty-two for a true trapezoid and twenty-three for a rectangle (uneven row).

These numbers themselves are theoretical, since certain banana trees have already been cut at ground level, once the stem has matured. There are actually nineteen tufts of leaves and two empty spaces which constitute the fourth row, and in the fifth, twenty tufts and one space – that is, from bottom to top: eight tufts of leaves, an empty space, twelve tufts of leaves.

Without bothering with the order in which the actually visible banana trees and the cut banana trees occur, the sixth row gives the following numbers: twenty-two, twenty-one, twenty, nineteen – which represent respectively the rectangle, the true trapezoid, the trapezoid with a curved edge and the same after subtracting the boles cut for the harvest.

And for the following rows: twenty-three, twenty-one, twenty-one, twenty-one. Twenty-two, twenty-one, twenty, twenty. Twenty-three, twenty-one, twenty, nineteen, etc...

On the log bridge that crosses the stream at the bottom edge of this patch, there is a man crouching: a native, wearing blue trousers and a colourless undershirt that leaves his shoulders bare. He is leaning towards the liquid surface, as if he were trying to see something at the bottom, which is scarcely possible, the water never being transparent enough despite its extreme shallowness.

On the near slope of the valley, a single patch runs uphill from the stream to the garden. Despite the rather slight declivity the slope appears to have, the banana trees are still easy to count here from the height of the veranda. As a matter of fact, the trees are very young in this zone, which has only recently been replanted. Not only is the regularity of the planting perfect here, but the trunks are no more than a foot and a half high, and the tufts of leaves that terminate them are still quite far apart from each other. Finally, the angle of the rows with the axis of the valley (about forty-five degrees) also favours their enumeration.

An oblique row begins at the log bridge, at the right, and reaches the left corner of the garden. It includes the thirty-six trees in its length. The alternate arrangement makes it possible to consider these same trees as being aligned in three other directions: first of all, the perpendicular to the first direction mentioned, then two others, also perpendicular to each other and forming angles of forty-five degrees with the first two. These last two rows are therefore respectively parallel and perpendicular to the axis of the valley – and to the lower edge of the garden.

The garden is, at present, only a square of naked earth, recently spaded, out of which are growing perhaps a dozen thin young orange trees a little shorter than a man, planed at A...'s orders.

The house does not occupy the whole width of the garden. Therefore it is isolated on all sides from the green mass of the banana trees.

Across the bare ground, in front of the west gable end, falls the warped shadow of the house. The shadow of the roof is linked to the shadow of the veranda by the oblique shadow of the corner column. The balustrade here forms a barely perforated strip, whereas the real distance between the balusters is scarcely smaller than the average thickness of the latter.

The balusters are of turned wood, with a median hip and two accessory smaller bulges, one at each end. The paint, which has almost completely disappeared from the top surface of the handrail, is also beginning to flake off the bulging portions of the balusters; they present, for the most part, a wide zone of naked wood halfway up the baluster, on the rounded part of the stomach, on the veranda side. Between the grey paint that remains, faded with age, and the wood greyed by the action of humidity, appear little reddish-brown surfaces – the natural colour of the wood – where it has been exposed by the recent fall of new flakes of paint. The whole balustrade is to be repainted bright yellow: that is what A… has decided.

The windows of her bedroom are still closed. However, the blinds which have replaced the panes of glass are opened as far as possible, thus making the interior of the room bright enough. A… is standing in front of the right-hand window, looking out through one of the chinks in the blinds towards the veranda.

The man is still motionless, bending over the muddy water on the earth-covered log bridge. He has not moved an inch: crouching, head lowered, forearms resting on his thighs, hands hanging between his knees.

In front of him, in the patch along the opposite bank of the little stream, several stems look ripe for harvesting. Several boles have already been cut in this sector. Their empty places appear with perfect distinctiveness in the series of geometrical alignments. But on closer inspection it is possible to distinguish the sizeable shoot, that will replace the severed banana tree, a few inches away from the old stump, already beginning to spoil the perfect regularity of the alternate planting.

From the other side of the house can be heard the noise of a truck coming up the road on the near slope of the valley.

A…'s silhouette, outlined in horizontal strips against the blind of her bedroom window, has now disappeared.

Having reached the level portion of the road, just above the rocky outcrop that marks the end of the plateau, the truck shifts gears and continues with a less muffled rumble.

Then the sound gradually fades as it drives off east, through the scorched brush dotted with motionless trees, towards the next plantation – Franck's.

The bedroom window – the one nearest the hallway – opens outwards. The upper part of A...'s body is framed within it. She says "Hello" in the playful tone of someone who has slept well and awakened in a good mood; or of someone who prefers not to show what she is thinking about, if anything, and always flashes the same smile on principle – the same smile, which can be interpreted as derision just as well as affection, or the total absence of any feeling whatever.

Besides, she has not only just woken up now. It is obvious she has already taken her shower. She is still wearing her dressing gown, but her lips are freshly made up – the lipstick the same colour as their natural colour, a trifle deeper, and her carefully brushed hair gleams in the light from the window when she turns her head, shifting the soft, heavy curls, whose black mass falls over the white silk of her shoulder.

She goes to the heavy chest against the rear partition. She opens the top drawer to take out a small object, and turns back towards the light. On the log bridge, the crouching native has disappeared. There is no one visible around the house. No cutting crew is working in this sector for the moment.

A... is sitting at the little work table against the wall to her right, that separates the bedroom from the hallway. She leans forwards over some long and painstaking task: mending an extremely fine stocking, polishing her nails, a tiny pencil drawing... But A... never draws: to mend a run in her stocking she would have moved nearer the daylight;

if she needed a table to do her nails on, she would not have chosen this one.

Despite the apparent immobility of her head and shoulders, a series of jolts disturbs the black mass of her hair. From time to time she straightens up and seems to lean back to judge her work from a distance. Her hand rising slowly, she puts into place a short curl that has emerged from this shifting mass. The hand lingers as it rearranges the waves of hair, the tapering fingers bend and straighten, one after the other, quickly though without abruptness, the movement communicating itself from one to the other continuously, as if they were driven by the same mechanism.

Leaning over again, she has now resumed her interrupted task. The lustrous hair gleams with reddish highlights in the hollow of the curls. Slight quivers, quickly absorbed, run through the hair from one shoulder to the other, without its being possible to see the rest of the body stir at all.

On the veranda in front of the office windows, Franck is sitting in his customary place, on one of the chairs of local manufacture. Only these three have been brought out this morning. They are arranged as usual: the first two next to each other under the window, the third slightly to one side, on the other side of the coffee table.

A... has gone to get the glasses, the soda water and the cognac herself. She sets a tray with the two bottles and the three big glasses down at the table. Having uncorked the cognac, she turns towards Franck and looks at him, while she begins making his drink. But Franck, instead of watching the rising level of the alcohol, fixes his eyes a little too high, on A...'s face. She has arranged her hair into a low knot whose skilful waves seem about to come undone; some hidden pins must be keeping it firmer than it looks.

Franck's voice has uttered an exclamation: "Hey there! That's much too much!" or else: "Stop! That's much too much!" or, "Ten times too much," "Half again too much," etc... He holds up his right hand beside his head, the fingers slightly apart. A... begins to laugh.

"You should have stopped me sooner."

"But I didn't see..." Franck protests.

"Well, then," she answers, "you should keep your eye on the glass."

They look at each other without adding another word. Franck widens his smile, which wrinkles up the corners of his eyes. He opens his mouth as if he were going to say something, but he doesn't say anything. A...'s features, from a point three quarters of the way behind her, reveal nothing.

After several minutes – or several seconds – both are still in the same position. Franck's face, as well as his whole body, is virtually petrified. He is wearing shorts and a short-sleeved khaki shirt, whose shoulder straps and buttoned pockets have a vaguely military look. Over his rough cotton knee socks he wears tennis shoes coated with a thick layer of white shoe polish, cracked at the places where the canvas bends with the foot.

A... is about to pour the soda into the three glasses lined up on the coffee table. She distributes the first two, then, holding the third one in her hand, sits down in the empty chair beside Franck. He has already begun drinking.

"Is it cold enough?" A... asks him. "The bottle just came out of the refrigerator."

Franck nods and drinks another mouthful.

"There's ice if you want it," A... says. And without waiting for an answer she calls the boy.

There is a silence, during which the boy should appear on the veranda at the corner of the house. But no one comes.

Franck looks at A..., as if he expected her to call again, or stand up, or reach some decision. She makes a sudden face towards the balustrade.

"He doesn't hear," she says. "One of us had better go."

Neither she nor Franck moves. On A...'s face, turned in profile towards the corner of the veranda, there is neither smile nor expectation now, nor a sign of encouragement. Franck stares at the tiny bubbles clinging to the sides of his glass, which he is holding in front of his eyes at very close range.

One mouthful is enough to tell that this drink is not cold enough; Franck has still not answered one way or the other, though he has taken two already. Besides, only one bottle comes from the refrigerator: the soda, whose greenish sides are coated with a faint film of dew, where a hand with tapering fingers has left its print.

The cognac is always kept in the sideboard. A..., who brings out the ice bucket at the same time as the glasses every day, has not done so today.

"It's not worth bothering about,' Franck says.

To get to the pantry, the easiest way is to cross the house. Once across the threshold, a sensation of coolness accompanies the half-darkness. To the right, the office door is ajar.

The light, rubber-soled shoes make no sound on the hallway tiles. The door turns on its hinges without squeaking. The office floor is tiled too. The three windows are closed and their blinds are only half open, to keep the noonday heat out of the room.

Two of the windows overlook the central section of the veranda. The first, to the right, shows through its lowest chink, between the last two slats of wood, the black head of hair – at least the top part of it.

A… is sitting upright and motionless in her armchair. She is looking out over the valley in front of them. She is not speaking. Franck, invisible on her left, is also silent, or else speaking in a very low voice.

Although the office – like the bedrooms and the bathroom – opens onto the hallway, the hallway itself ends at the dining room, with no door between. The table is set for three. A… has probably just had the boy add Franck's place, since she was not supposed to be expecting any guest for lunch today.

The three plates are arranged as usual, each in the centre of one of the sides of the square table. The fourth side, where there is no place set, is the one next to about six feet of the bare partition, where the light paint shows the traces of the squashed centipede.

In the pantry the boy is already taking the ice cubes out of their trays. A pitcher full of water, set on the floor, has been used to heat the backs of the metal trays. He looks up and smiles broadly.

He would scarcely have had time to go and take A…'s orders on the veranda and return here (outside the house) with the necessary objects.

"Misses, she has said to bring the ice," he announces in the sing-song voice of the black people, which detaches certain syllables by emphasizing them too much, sometimes in the middle of words.

To a vague question as to when he received this order, he answers: "Now," which furnishes no satisfactory indication. She may just have asked him when she went to get the tray.

Only the boy could confirm this. But he sees in the awkwardly put question only a request to hurry.

"Right away I bring," he says.

He speaks well enough, but he does not always understand what is wanted of him. A..., however, managed to make herself understood without any difficulty.

From the pantry door, the dining-room wall seems to have no spot on it. No sound of conversation can be heard from the veranda at the other end of the hallway.

To the left, the office door has remained wide open this time. But the slats of the blind are too sharply slanted to permit what is outside to be seen from the doorway.

It is only at a distance of less than a yard that the elements of a discontinuous landscape appear in the successive intervals, parallel chinks separated by the wider slats of grey wood: the turned-wood balusters, the empty chair, the coffee table where a full glass is standing beside the tray holding the two bottles, and then the top part of the head of black hair, which at this moment turns towards the right, where above the table shows a bare forearm, dark brown in colour, and its paler hand holding the ice bucket. A...'s voice thanks the boy. The brown hand disappears. The shiny metal bucket, immediately frosted over, remains where it has been set on the tray beside the two bottles.

The knot of A...'s hair, seen at such close range from behind, seems to be extremely complicated. It is difficult to follow the convolutions of different strands: several solutions seem possible at some places, and in others, none.

Instead of serving the ice, A... continues to look out over the valley. Of the garden earth, cut up into vertical slices by the balustrade, and into horizontal strips by the blinds,

26

there remains only a series of little squares representing a very small part of the surface – perhaps a ninth.

The knot of A...'s hair is at least as confusing when it appears in profile. She is sitting to Franck's left. (It is always that way: on Franck's right for coffee or cocktails, on his left during the meals in the dining room.) She still keeps her back to the windows, but it is now from these windows that the daylight comes. These windows are conventional ones, with panes of glass: facing north, they never receive direct sunlight.

The windows are closed. No sound penetrates inside when a silhouette passes in front of one of them, walking alongside the house from the kitchen towards the sheds. Cut off below the knee, it was a black man wearing shorts, undershirt and an old soft hat, walking with a quick, loose gait, probably barefoot. His felt hat, shapeless and faded, is unforgettable, and should make him immediately recognizable among all the workers on the plantation. He is not, however.

The second window is located further back, in relation to the table; to see it requires a pivoting of the upper part of the body. But no one is outlined against it, either because the man in the hat has already passed it, or because he has just stopped, or has suddenly changed his direction. His disappearance is hardly astonishing, it merely makes his first appearance curious.

"It's all in the mind, things like that," Franck says.

The African novel again provides the subject of their conversation.

"People say it's the climate, but that doesn't mean anything."

"Malarial attacks..."

here's quinine."

"And your head buzzing all day long."

The moment has come to enquire after Christiane's health. Franck replies by a gesture of the hand: a rise followed by a slower fall that becomes quite vague, while the fingers close over a piece of bread set down beside his plate. At the same time his lower lip is projected and the chin quickly turned towards A..., who must have asked the same question a little earlier.

The boy comes in through the open pantry door, holding a large shallow bowl in both hands.

A... has not made the remarks which Franck's gesture was supposed to introduce. There remains one remedy: to ask after the child. The same gesture – or virtually the same – is made, which again concludes with A...'s silence.

"Still the same," Franck says.

Going in the opposite direction behind the panes, the felt hat passes by again. The quick, loose gait has not changed. But the opposite orientation of the face conceals the latter altogether.

Behind the thick glass, which is perfectly clean, there is only the gravel courtyard, then, rising towards the road and the edge of the plateau, the green mass of the banana trees. The flaws in the glass produce shifting circles in their unvarying foliage.

The light itself has a somewhat greenish cast as it falls on the dining room, the black hair with the improbable convolutions, the cloth on the table and the bare partition where a dark stain, just opposite A..., stands out on the pale, dull, even paint.

The details of the stain have to be seen from quite close range, turning towards the pantry door, if its origin is to be distinguished. The image of the squashed centipede then appears not as a whole, but composed of fragments distinct enough to leave no doubt. Several pieces of the body or its appendages are outlined without any blurring, and remain reproduced with the fidelity of an anatomical drawing: one of the antennae, two curved mandibles, the head and the first joint, half of the second, three large legs. Then come the other parts, less precise: sections of legs and the partial form of a body convulsed into a question mark.

It is at this hour that the lighting in the dining room is the most favourable. From the other side of the square table where the places have not yet been set, one of the French windows, whose panes are darkened by no dust at all, is open on the courtyard, which is also reflected in the glass.

Between the two window leaves, as through the half-open right one, is framed the left side of the courtyard, where the tarpaulin-covered truck is parked, its hood facing the northern sector of the banana plantation. Under the tarpaulin is a raw wood case, marked with large black letters painted in reverse through a stencil.

In the left window leaf the reflection is brighter, though deeper in hue. But it is distorted by flaws in the glass, the circular crescent-shaped spots of verdure, the same colours as the banana trees, occurring in the middle of the courtyard in front of the sheds.

Nicked by one of the moving rings of foliage, the big blue sedan nevertheless remains quite recognizable, as well as A...'s dress, where she is standing next to the car.

She is leaning towards the door. If the window has been lowered – which is likely – A... may have put her face into the opening above the seat. In straightening up, she runs the risk of disarranging her hair against the edge of the window, and seeing her hair spread out and fall over the driver behind the wheel.

The latter is here again for dinner, affable and smiling. He drops into one of the leather chairs without anyone's telling him which, and utters his usual exclamation as to their comfort.

"That feels good!"

His white shirt makes a paler spot in the darkness, against the wall of the house.

In order not to risk spilling the contents in the darkness, A... has come as close as possible to Franck's armchair, carefully holding his glass in her right hand. She rests her other hand on the arm of his chair and leans towards him, so close that their heads touch. He murmurs a few words, probably thanking her. But the words are drowned out by the deafening racket of the crickets that rises on all sides.

At table, once the arrangement of the lamps has been shifted so that the guests are in less direct a light, the conversation continues on familiar subjects, with the same phrases.

Franck's truck has had engine trouble on the middle of the hill, between the forty-mile marker – where the road leaves the plain – and the first village. It was a police car which passed the truck and then stopped at the plantation to inform Franck. When the latter reached the spot two hours later, he did not find his truck at the place indicated, but much lower down, the driver having tried to start the motor in reverse, at the risk of crashing into a tree if he missed one of the turns.

Expecting any results at all from such a method was ridiculous anyway. The carburettor would have to be completely dismantled all over again. Luckily Franck had brought along a snack lunch, for he didn't get home until three thirty. He has decided to replace the truck as soon as possible, and it's the last time – he says – that he will buy old military equipment.

"You think you're getting a bargain, but in the long run it costs much more."

He now expects to buy a new truck. He is going down to the port himself at the first opportunity and will meet with the sales agents of the chief makes, so that he can find out the exact prices, the various advantages, delivery time, etc…

If he had a little more experience, he would know that new machines should not be entrusted to the black drivers, who wreck them just as fast, if not faster.

"When do you think you'll be going down?" A… asks.

"I don't know…" They look at each other, their glances meeting above the platter Franck is holding in one hand six inches above the table top. "Maybe next week."

"I have to go to town too," A… says; "I have a lot of shopping to do."

"Well, I'll be glad to take you. If we leave early, we can be back the same night."

He sets the platter down on his left and begins helping himself. A… turns back so that she is looking straight ahead.

"A centipede!" she says in a more restrained voice, in the silence that has just fallen.

Franck looks up again. Following the direction of A…'s motionless gaze, he turns his head to the other side, towards his right.

On the light-coloured paint of the partition opposite A…, a common *Scutigera* of average size (about as long as

...as appeared, easily seen despite the dim light. It is
...ng for the moment, but the orientation of its body
indicates the path which cuts across the panel diagonally:
coming from the skirting board on the hallway side and
heading towards the corner of the ceiling. The creature
is easy to identify thanks to the development of its legs,
especially on the posterior portion. On closer examination
the swaying movement of the antennae at the other end can
be discerned.

A... has not moved since her discovery: sitting very
straight in her chair, her hands resting flat on the cloth on
either side of her plate. Her eyes are wide, staring at the
wall. Her mouth is not quite closed, and may be quivering
imperceptibly.

It is not unusual to encounter different kinds of centipedes
after dark in this already old wooden house. And this kind
is not one of the largest; it is far from being one of the
most venomous. A... does her best, but does not manage
to look away, nor to smile at the joke about her aversion to
centipedes.

Franck, who has said nothing, is looking at A... again.
Then he stands up noiselessly, holding his napkin in his
hand. He wads it into a ball and approaches the wall.

A... seems to be breathing a little faster, but this may be
an illusion. Her left hand gradually closes over her knife.
The delicate antennae accelerate their alternate swaying.

Suddenly the creature hunches its body and begins de-
scending diagonally towards the ground as fast as its long
legs can go, while the wadded napkin falls on it, faster
still.

The hand with the tapering fingers has clenched around
the knife handle, but the features of the face have lost none

of their rigidity. Franck lifts the napkin away from the wall and with his foot continues to squash something on the tiles, against the skirting board.

About a yard higher, the paint is marked with a dark shape, a tiny arc twisted into a question mark, blurred on one side, in places surrounded by more tenuous signs, from which A... has still not taken her eyes.

The brush descends the length of the loose hair with a faint noise something between the sound of a breath and a crackle. No sooner has it reached the bottom than it quickly rises again towards the head, where the whole surface of its bristles sinks in before gliding down over the black mass again. The brush is a bone-coloured oval whose short handle disappears almost entirely in the hand firmly gripping it.

Half of the hair hangs down the back, the other hand pulls the other half over the shoulder. The head leans to the right, offering the hair more readily to the brush. Each time the latter lands at the top of its cycle behind the nape of the neck, the head leans further to the right, then rises again with an effort, while the right hand, holding the brush, moves away in the opposite direction. The left hand, which loosely confines the hair between the wrist, the palm and the fingers, releases it for a second, and then closes on it again, gathering the strands together with a firm, mechanical gesture, while the brush continues its course to the extreme tips of the hair. The sound which gradually varies from one end to the other is at this point nothing more than a dry, faint crackling, whose last sputters occur once the brush, leaving the longest hair, is already moving up the ascending part of the cycle, describing a swift curve in the air which brings it above the neck, where the hair lies flat on the back of the head and reveals the white streak of a parting.

To the left of this parting, the other half of the black hair hangs loosely to the waist in supple waves. Still further to the left, the face shows only a faint profile. But beyond is the surface of the mirror, which reflects the image of the whole face from the front, the eyes – doubtless unnecessary for brushing – directed ahead, as is natural.

Thus A...'s eyes should meet the wide-open window which overlooks the west gable end. Facing in this direction, she is brushing her hair in front of the dressing table provided specially with a vertical mirror, which reflects her gaze behind her, towards the bedroom's third window, the central portion of the veranda and the slope of the valley.

The second window, which looks south like this third one, is nearer the south-west corner of the house; it too is wide open. Through it can be seen the side of the dressing table, the edge of the mirror, the left profile of the face, the loose hair which hangs over the shoulder and the left arm which is bent back to reach the right half of the hair.

Since the nape of the neck is bent diagonally to the right, the face is slightly turned towards the window. On the grey-streaked marble table top are arranged jars and bottles of various sizes and shapes; nearer the front lies a large tortoiseshell comb and another brush, this one of wood with a longer handle, which is lying with its black bristles facing up.

A... must have just washed her hair, otherwise she would not be bothering to brush it in the middle of the day. She has interrupted her movements, having finished the side perhaps. Nevertheless, she does not change the position of her arms or move the upper part of her body, as she turns her face all the way around towards the window at her left to look out at the veranda, the openwork balustrade and the opposite slope of the valley.

The foreshortened shadow of the column supporting the corner of the roof falls across the veranda flagstones towards the first window, that of the gable end, but it is far from reaching it, for the sun is still too high in the sky. The gable end of the house is entirely in the shadow of the roof; as for the western part of the veranda running the length of this gable end, an unbroken sunny strip scarcely a yard wide lies between the shadow of the roof and the shadow of the balustrade.

It is in front of this window, inside the bedroom, that the varnished mahogany-and-marble dressing table has been set; there is always a specimen of such pieces in these colonial-style houses.

The back of the mirror is a panel of rougher wood, also reddish, but dark, oval in shape and with a chalk inscription almost entirely erased. To the right, A...'s face, which is now bent towards her left so she can brush the other half of her hair, shows one eye staring straight ahead of her, as is natural, towards the open window and the green mass of the banana trees.

At the end of the western side of the veranda opens the outside door of the pantry; the pantry opens onto the dining room, where it stays cool all afternoon. On the bare wall between the pantry door and the hallway, the stain formed by the remains of the centipede is scarcely visible because of the oblique light. The table is set for three; three places occupy three sides of the square table: the buffet side, the window side and the side towards the centre of the long room. The other half of this room forms a living room on the other side of an imaginary central line between the hall doorway and the door opening onto the courtyard. From the courtyard it is easy to reach the sheds where the native overseer has his office.

But this living room – or the side of the shed through a window – can be seen only from Franck's place at the table: back to the sideboard.

At present this place is empty. The chair is nevertheless put in the right spot, the plate and silver are in their places too, but there is nothing between the edge of the table and the back of the chair – which shows its trimming of thick straw bound in a cross – and the plate is clean and shiny, surrounded by the usual knives and forks, as at the beginning of the meal.

A…, who has finally decided to have the lunch served without waiting for the guest any longer, since he hasn't come, is sitting rigid and silent in her own place, in front of the windows. Though the discomfort of this location, with the light behind her, seems flagrant, it has been chosen by A… once and for all. She eats with an extreme economy of gestures, not turning her head right or left, her eyes squinting slightly, as if she were trying to discover a stain on the bare wall in front of her – where, however, the immaculate paint offers not the slightest object to her gaze.

After clearing away the hors d'oeuvre but not bothering to change the unused plate of the absent guest, the boy comes in again through the open pantry door, holding a wide, shallow platter in both hands. A… doesn't even turn to give it her usual "mistress of the house" glance. Without a word, the boy sets the platter down on the white cloth to her right.

It contains a yellowish purée, probably of yams, from which rises a thin trail of steam, which suddenly curves, flattens out and vanishes without leaving a trace, reappearing at once – long, delicate and vertical – high above the table.

In the middle of the table there is already another untouched platter on which, against a background of brown sauce, are arranged three small roasted birds, one next to the other.

The boy has withdrawn, silent as ever. A... suddenly decides to look away from the bare wall, and now considers the two platters, one on her right and one in front of her. Having grasped the appropriate spoon, she helps herself with careful and precise gestures: the smallest of the three birds, then a little of the purée. Then she picks up the platter at her right and sets it down on her left; the large spoon has remained in it.

She begins meticulously cutting up the bird on her plate. Despite the smallness of the object, she takes apart the limbs as if she were performing an anatomical demonstration, cuts up the body at the joints, detaches the flesh from the skeleton with the point of her knife while holding the pieces down with her fork, without applying force, without ever having to repeat the same gesture, without even seeming to be accomplishing a difficult or unaccustomed task. These birds, it is true, are served frequently.

When she has finished, she raises her head, looking straight ahead of her, and remains motionless again, while the boy takes out the plates covered with the tiny bones, then the two platters, one of which still contains a third roasted bird, the one meant for Franck.

The latter's place remains as it was until the end of the meal. He has probably been delayed, as is not infrequently the case, by some incident occurring on his plantation, since he would not have put off this lunch for any possible ailments of his wife or child.

Although it is unlikely that the guest should come now, perhaps A... is still expecting to hear the sound of a car coming down the slope from the highway. But through the dining-room windows, of which at least one is half open, no motor hum or any other noise can be heard at this hour of the day, when all work is interrupted and even the animals fall silent in the heat.

The corner window has both leaves open – at least partly. The one on the right is only ajar, so that it still covers at least half of the window opening. The left leaf, on the other hand, is pushed back towards the wall, but not all the way either – it is scarcely more than perpendicular, in fact, to the window sash. The window therefore shows three panels of equal height which are of adjoining widths: in the centre, the opening and, on each side, a glass area comprising three panes. In all three are framed fragments of the same landscape: the gravel courtyard and the green mass of the banana trees.

The windows are perfectly clean and, in the right-hand leaf, the landscape is only slightly affected by the flaws in the glass, which give a few shifting nuances to the too uniform surfaces. But in the left leaf, the reflected image, darker although more brilliant, is plainly distorted – circular or crescent-shaped spots of verdure the same colour as the banana trees – moving in the middle of the courtyard in front of the sheds.

Franck's big blue sedan, which has just appeared here, is also nicked by one of these shifting rings of foliage, as is A...'s white dress when she gets out of the car.

She leans towards the door. If the window has been lowered – which is likely – A... may have put her face into the opening above the seat. In straightening up, she runs the risk of disarranging her hair against the edge of the window, causing it to spread out and fall – all the more readily mussed since it has recently been washed – over the driver still behind the wheel.

But she draws away unscathed from the blue car, whose motor, which has been idling, now fills the courtyard with a louder hum, and after a last look behind her, heads alone, with her decisive gait, towards the centre door of the house which opens directly into the living room.

Opposite this door opens the hallway, with no door between it and the living room/dining room. Doors occur one after another on each side; the last to the left, that of the office, is not completely closed. The door moves without creaking on its well-oiled hinges; it then returns to its initial position with the same discretion.

At the other end of the house, the entrance door, opened with less care, has closed again; then the faint distinct sound of high heels on tiles crosses the living room/dining room and approaches down the length of the hallway.

The steps stop in front of the office door, but it is the door opposite, to the bedroom, which is opened, then shut again.

Symmetrical to those of the bedroom, the three windows of the office have their blinds more than half lowered at this hour. Thus the office is plunged into a dimness which makes it difficult to judge distances. Lines are just as distinct, but the succession of planes gives no impression of depth, so that hands instinctively reach out in front of the body to measure the space more precisely.

The room is fortunately not very full of furniture: files and shelves against the walls, a few chairs, and then the huge desk, which fills the entire area between the two windows facing south, one of which – on the right, nearer the hallway – reveals through the chinks between its wood slats the silhouette, in luminous parallel stripes, of the tables and chairs on the veranda.

On the corner of the dressing table sands a little mother-of-pearl-inlaid frame with a photograph taken by a street photographer during the first holiday in Europe after the African trip.

In front of the façade of a large "modern" café, A... is sitting on a complicated wrought-iron chair whose arms and back, in bracketed spirals, seem less comfortable than spectacular. But A..., from her manner of sitting on the chair, looks as natural as ever, though without the slightest slackness.

She has turned slightly to smile at the photographer, as if to authorize him to take this candid shot. Her bare arm, at the same moment, has not changed the gesture it was making to set the glass down on the table beside her.

But it was not to put ice in it, for she does not reach for the ice bucket of shiny metal which is immediately frosted over.

Motionless, she stares at the valley in front of them. She says nothing. Franck, invisible to her left, also says nothing. Perhaps she has heard some abnormal sound behind her and is about to make some movement without discernible preparation, which would permit her to look towards the blind quite by chance.

The window facing east, on the other side of the office, is not merely a window, like the corresponding one in the bedroom, but a French door which permits direct access to the veranda without passing through the hallway.

This part of the veranda receives the morning sun, the only kind that need not be avoided by some protection or other. In the almost cool air after daybreak, the song of birds replaces that of the nocturnal crickets, and resembles it, although less regular and sometimes embellished with slightly more musical sounds. As for the birds themselves, they are no more in evidence than the crickets were, remaining in hiding under the clusters of wide green leaves on all sides of the house.

In the zone of naked earth which separates the house from the trees, where at regular intervals the young orange trees are planted – thin stems with occasional dark-coloured foliage – the ground sparkles with innumerable dew-covered webs spun by tiny spiders between the clods of spaded earth.

To the right, this part of the veranda adjoins the end of the living room. But it is always outdoors, in front of the southern façade – with a view over the entire valley – that the morning meal is served. On the coffee table, near the single chair brought here by the boy, the coffee pot and the cup are already arranged. A… is not up yet, at this hour. The windows of her bedroom are still closed.

In the hollow of the valley, on the log bridge that crosses the little stream, there is a man crouching, facing the opposite hillside. He is a native, wearing blue trousers and a colourless undershirt that leaves his shoulders bare. He is leaning towards the liquid surface as if he were trying to see something in the muddy water.

In front of him, on the opposite bank, stretches a trapezoid-shaped patch, the side along the bank curved; all of those banana trees have been harvested more or less recently. It is easy to count their stumps, the cut trunks leaving a short stub with a disc-shaped scar, white or yellowish depending upon its freshness. Counting by rows, there are: from left to right twenty-three, twenty-two, twenty-one, twenty-one, twenty, twenty-one, twenty, twenty, etc…

Beside each white disc, but in various directions, the replacing sprout has grown. Depending on the precocity of the first stem, this new plant is now between a foot and a half and a yard in height.

A… has just brought out the glasses, the two bottles and the ice bucket. She begins serving: the cognacs in the three glasses, then the soda, and finally three transparent ice cubes, each of which imprisons a bundle of silver needles in its heart.

"We'll be leaving early," Franck says.

"What do you mean – early?"

"Six o'clock, if you can make it."

"Six! My goodness…"

"Too early for you?"

"Oh no." She laughs. Then after a pause, "In fact, it'll be fun."

They sip their drinks.

"If all goes well," Franck says, "we'll be in town by ten and have an hour or two before lunch."

"Yes, of course. I'd prefer that too," A… says.

They sip their drinks.

Then they change the subject. Now both of them have finished the books they have been reading for some time; their remarks can therefore refer to the book as a whole: that is, both to the outcome and to the earlier episodes (subjects of past conversations) to which this outcome gives a new significance, or to which it adds a complementary meaning.

They have never made the slightest judgement as to the novel's value, speaking instead of the scenes, events and characters as if they were real: a place they might remember (located in Africa, moreover), people they might have known, or whose adventures someone might have told them. Their discussions have never touched on the verisimilitude, the coherence or the quality of the narrative. On the other hand, they frequently blame the heroes for certain acts or characteristics, as they would in the case of mutual friends.

They also sometimes deplore the coincidences of the plot, saying that "things don't happen that way", and then they construct a different probable outcome starting from a new supposition – "if it weren't for that". Other possibilities are offered, during the course of the book, which lead to different endings. The variations are extremely numerous; the variations of these, still more so. They seem to enjoy multiplying these choices, exchanging smiles, carried away by their enthusiasm, probably a little intoxicated by this proliferation...

"But that's it, he was just unlucky enough to have come home earlier that day, and no one could have guessed he would."

Thus Franck sweeps away in a single gesture all the suppositions they had just constructed together. It's no use making up contrary possibilities, since things are the way they are: reality stays the same.

They sip their drinks. In the three glasses, the ice cubes have now altogether disappeared. Franck inspects the gold liquid remaining in the bottom of his glass. He turns it to one side, then the other, amusing himself by detaching the little bubbles clinging to the sides.

"Still," he says, "it started out well." He turns towards A… for her support: "We left on schedule and were driving along without any trouble. It wasn't even ten o'clock when we reached town."

Franck has stopped talking. A… continues, as if to encourage him to resume.

"And you didn't notice anything funny that whole day, did you?"

"No, nothing at all. In a way, it would have been better if we had the trouble with the engine right away, before lunch. Not on the trip, but in town, before lunch. It would have made it harder for me to do some of my errands – the ones that weren't in the middle of town – but at least I would have had time to find a garage that could have made the repairs during the afternoon."

"Because it really wasn't a very big job," A… puts in questioningly.

"No, it was nothing."

Franck looks at his glass. After a rather long pause, and although this time no one has asked him anything, he continues explaining:

"The moment we started back after dinner, the engine wouldn't start. It was too late to do anything, of course: every garage was closed. All we could do was wait until morning."

The sentences followed one another, each in its place, connecting logically. The measured, uniform pace was like that of a witness offering testimony, or a recitation.

"Even so," A… says, "you thought you could fix it yourself, at first. At least you tried. But you're not much of a mechanic, are you?"

She smiles as she says these last words. They look at each other. He smiles too. Then slowly, his smile becomes a kind of grimace. She, on the other hand, keeps her look of amused serenity.

Yet Franck can't be unused to makeshift repairs, since his truck is always having engine trouble...

"Yes," he says, "I'm beginning to know *that* motor pretty well. But the car hasn't given me trouble very often."

As a matter of fact, there has never been another incident with the big blue sedan, which is, moreover, almost new.

"There has to be a first time for everything," Franck answers. Then after a pause: "It was just my unlucky day..."

A little gesture of his right hand – rising, then falling more slowly – has just come to an end on the strip of leather that constitutes the arm of the chair. Franck's face is drawn; his smile has not reappeared since the grimace of a few minutes ago. His body seems to be stuck to the chair.

"Unlucky, maybe, but it wasn't a tragedy," A... replies, in a casual tone that contrasts with that of her companion. "If we had access to a telephone, the delay wouldn't have mattered at all, but with these plantations isolated in the jungle, what could we do? In any case, its better than being stuck on the road in the middle of the night!"

It's better than having an accident too. It was only a piece of bad luck, without consequences, an incident of no seriousness, one of the minor inconveniences of colonial life.

"I think I'll be getting along," Franck says.

He has just stopped here to drop A... off on his way home. He doesn't want to waste any more time. Christiane must be wondering what's become of him, and Franck is eager to reassure her. He stands up with sudden energy and sets down on the coffee table the glass he has emptied at one gulp.

"Till next time," A... says, without leaving her own chair, "and thank you."

Franck makes a vague gesture with his arm, a conventional protest. A... insists:

"No, really! I've been on your neck for two days."

"Not at all. I'm terribly sorry to have given you a night like that in that miserable hotel."

He has taken two steps, he stops before turning down the hallway that crosses the house, he half turns around: "And please forgive me for being such a bad mechanic." The same grimace, faster now, slides across his face. He disappears into the house.

His steps echo over the tiles of the hallway. He had leather-soled shoes on today, and a white suit that has been wrinkled by the trip.

When the door at the other end of the house has opened and closed again, A... gets up too and leaves the veranda by the same door. But she goes to her bedroom at once, closing and locking the door behind her, making the latch click loudly. In the courtyard, in front of the northern façade of the house, the sound of a motor starting up is immediately followed by the shrill protest of gears forced to make too fast a getaway. Franck has not said what kind of repairs his car had needed.

A... closes the windows of her bedroom, which have stayed wide open all morning, lowering the blinds one after the other. She is going to change, to take a shower, probably, after the long dusty road.

The bathroom opens off the bedroom. A second door opens onto the hallway; the bolt is closed from inside, with a swift gesture that makes a loud click.

The next room, still on the same side of the hallway, is a bedroom, much smaller than A...'s, which contains a single bed. Six feet further, the hallway ends at the dining room.

The table is set for one person. A...'s place will have to be added.

On the bare wall, the traces of the squashed centipede are still perfectly visible. Nothing has been done to clean off the stain, for fear of spoiling the handsome, dull finish, probably not washable.

The table is set for three, according to the usual arrangement... Franck and A..., sitting in their usual places, are talking about the trip to town they intend to make together during the following week, she for various shopping errands, he to find out about a new truck he wants to buy.

They have already settled the time for their departure, as well as for their return, calculated the approximate duration of the time on the road in each direction, estimated the time they will have for their errands, including lunch and dinner, in town. They have not specified whether they will take their meals separately or if they will meet to have them together. But the question hardly comes up, since only one restaurant serves decent meals to travellers passing through town. It is only natural that they will meet there, especially for dinner, since they must start back immediately afterwards.

It is also natural that A... would want to take advantage of this present opportunity to get to town, which she prefers to the solution of a banana truck – virtually impracticable on such a long road – and that she should furthermore prefer Franck's company to that of some native driver, no matter how great the mechanical ability she attributes to the latter. As for the other occasions which permit her to make the trip under acceptable circumstances, they are indisputably rather infrequent, even exceptional, if not nonexistent, unless there are serious reasons to justify a categorical insistence on her part, which always more or less upsets the proper functioning of the plantation.

This time, she has asked for nothing, nor indicated the precise nature of the purchases which motivated her expedition. There was no special reason to give, once a friend's car was available to pick her up at home and bring her back the same night. The most surprising thing of all, upon consideration, is that such an arrangement should not already have been made, one day or another.

Franck has been eating without speaking for several minutes. It is A..., whose plate is empty, her fork and knife laid across it side by side, who resumes the conversation, asking after Christiane, whom fatigue (due to the heat, she thinks) has kept from coming with her husband on several occasions recently.

"It's always the same," Franck answers. "I've asked her to come down to the port with us, for a change of scene. But she didn't want to, on account of the child."

"Not to mention," A... says, "that it's much hotter down on the coast."

"More humid, yes," Franck agrees.

Then five or six remarks are exchanged as to the respective doses of quinine necessary down on the coast and up here. Franck returns to the ill effects quinine produces on the heroine of the African novel they are reading. The conversation is thus left to the central events of the story in question.

On the other side of the closed window, in the dusty courtyard whose rough gravel gathers into heaps, the truck has its hood turned towards the house. With the exception of this detail, it is parked precisely in the spot intended for it: that is, it is framed between the lower and middle panes of the right-hand window leaf, against the inner jamb, the little crosspiece cutting its outline horizontally into two masses of equal size.

Through the open pantry door, A... comes into the dining room towards the table where the meal has been served. She has come around by the veranda in order to speak to the cook, whose voluble, sing-song voice rose just a moment ago in the kitchen.

A... has changed her clothes after taking a shower, she has put on the light-coloured, close-fitting dress Christiane says is unsuitable for a tropical climate. She is going to sit down at her place, her back to the window, before the setting the boy has added for her. She unfolds her napkin on her knees and begins to help herself, her left hand raising the cover of the still-warm platter that had already been served while she was in the bathroom, but still remains in the middle of the table.

She says: "The trip made me hungry."

Then she asks about the incidents occurring on the plantation during her absence. The expression she uses ("What's new?") is spoken in a light tone, with an animation indicating no particular attention. Besides, there is nothing new.

Yet A... seems to have an unusual desire to talk. She feels – she says – that a lot of things must have happened during this period of time, which, for her part, was busily filled.

On the plantation too this time has been well employed, but only by the usual series of activities, which are always the same, for the most part. She herself, questioned as to her news, limits her remarks to four or five pieces of information already known: the road is still being repaired for five or six miles after the first village, the *Cap Saint-Jean* was in the harbour waiting for its cargo, the work on the new post office has not advanced much in the last three months. The municipal road service is still unsatisfactory, etc...

She helps herself again. It would be better to put the truck in the shed, since no one is to use it at the beginning of the afternoon. The thick glass of the window nicks the body of the truck with a deep, rounded scallop behind the front wheel. Somewhat further down, isolated from the principle mass by a strip of gravel, a half-circle of painted metal is refracted more than a foot and a half from its real location. This aberrant piece can also be moved about as the observer pleases, changing its shape as well as its dimensions: it swells from right to left, shrinks in the opposite direction, becomes a crescent towards the bottom, a complete circle as it moves upwards, or else acquires a fringe (but this is a very limited, almost instantaneous position) of two concentric aureoles. Finally, with larger shifts, it melts into the main surface, or disappears with a sudden contraction.

A... tries talking a little more; she nevertheless does not describe the room where she spent the night – an uninteresting subject, she says, turning away her head, everyone knows that hotel, its discomfort and its patched mosquito netting.

It is at this moment that she notices the *Scutigera* on the bare wall in front of her. In an even tone of voice, as if in order not to frighten the creature, she says:

"A centipede!"

Franck looks up again. Following the direction of A...'s motionless gaze, he turns his head to the other side.

The animal is motionless in the centre of the panel, easily seen against the light-coloured paint, despite the dim light. Franck, who has said nothing, looks at A... again. Then he stands up noiselessly. A... moves no more than the centipede while Franck approaches the wall, his napkin wadded up in this hand.

The hand with tapering fingers has clenched into a fist on the white cloth.

Franck lifts the napkin away from the wall and continues to squash something on the tiles with his foot, against the skirting board. And he sits down in his place again, to the right of the lamp lit behind him on the sideboard.

When he passed in front of the lamp, his shadow swept over the table top, which it covered entirely for an instant. Then the boy comes in through the open door; he begins to clear the table in silence. A... asks him to serve the coffee on the veranda, as usual.

She and Franck, sitting in their chairs, continue a desultory discussion of which day would be most convenient for this little trip to town they have been planning since the evening before.

The subject is soon exhausted. Its interest does not diminish, but they find no new element to nourish it. The sentences become shorter, and limit themselves, for the most part, to repeating fragments of those spoken during these last two days, or even before.

After some final monosyllables, separated by increasingly longer pauses and ultimately no longer intelligible, they let the night triumph altogether.

Vague shapes indicated by the less intense obscurity of a light-coloured dress or shirt, they are sitting side by side, leaning back in their chairs, arms reposing on the elbow rests, occasionally making vague movements of small extent, no sooner moving from these original positions than returning to them, or perhaps not moving at all.

The crickets too have fallen silent.

There is only the shrill cry of some nocturnal carnivore to be heard from time to time, and the sudden buzzing of a beetle, the clink of a little porcelain cup being set on the coffee table.

Now the voice of the second driver reaches this central section of the veranda, coming from the direction of the sheds; it is singing a native tune with incomprehensible words, or even without words.

The sheds are located on the other side of the house, to the right of the large courtyard. The voice must therefore come around the corner occupied by the office and beneath the overhanging roof, which noticeably muffles it, though some sound can cross the room itself through the blinds (on the south façade and the east gable end).

But it is a voice that carries well, full and strong, though in a rather low register. It is flexible too, flowing easily from one note to another, then suddenly breaking off.

Because of the peculiar nature of this kind of melody, it is difficult to determine if the song is interrupted for some fortuitous reason – in relation, for instance, to the manual work the singer is performing at the same time – or whether the tune has come to its natural conclusion.

Similarly, when it begins again, it is just as sudden, as abrupt, starting on notes which hardly seem to constitute a beginning or a reprise.

At other places, however, something seems about to end; everything indicates this – a gradual cadence, tranquillity regained, the feeling that nothing remains to be said – but after the note which should be the last comes another one, without the least break in continuity, with the same ease, then another, and others following, and the hearer supposes himself transported into the heart of the poem... when at that point everything stops without warning.

A..., in the bedroom, again bends over the letter she is writing. The sheet of pale-blue paper in front of her has only a few lines on it at this point. A... adds three or four more words rather hastily, and holds her pen in the air above the paper. After a moment she raises her head again, while the song resumes from the direction of the sheds.

It is doubtless the same poem continuing. If the themes sometimes blur, they only recur somewhat later, all the more clearly, virtually identical. Yet these repetitions, these tiny variations, halts, regressions, can give rise to modifications – though barely perceptible – eventually moving quite far from the point of departure.

To hear better, A... has turned her head towards the open window next to her. In the hollow of the valley, work is under way to repair the log bridge over the little stream. The layer of earth has been removed from about a quarter of its width. The men are going to replace the termite-infested wood with new logs that still have their bark on, cut to the proper lengths beforehand – now lying across the road, just in front of the bridge. Instead of piling them up in an orderly fashion, the porters have thrown them down, and left them lying all over the place.

The first two logs are lying parallel to each other (and to the bank), the space between them equivalent to approximately twice their common diameter. A third cuts across them diagonally at about a third of the way across their length. The next, perpendicular to this latter, touches its end; its other end almost touches the last log, which forms a loose V with it, its point not quite closed. But this fifth log is also parallel to the two first logs, and to the direction of the stream the little bridge is built over.

How much time has passed since the bridge underpinnings last had to be repaired? The logs, supposedly treated against termite action, must have received defective treatment. Sooner or later, of course, these earth-covered logs, periodically doused by the rising stream, are liable to be infected by insects. It is possible to protect over long periods of time only structures built far off the ground, as in the case of the house, for instance.

In the bedroom, A... has continued her letter in her delicate, close-set, regular handwriting. The page is now half full. But she slowly raises her head, and begins to turn it gradually but steadily towards the open window.

There are five workmen at the bridge, and as many new logs. All the men are now crouching in the same position: forearms resting on their thighs, hands hanging between their knees. They are facing each other, two on the right bank, three on the left. They are probably discussing how they are going to complete their job, or else are resting a little before the effort, tired from having carried the logs this far. In any case, they are perfectly motionless.

In the banana plantation behind them, a trapeze-shaped patch stretches uphill, and since no stems have been harvested in it yet, the regularity of the trees' alternate arrangement is still absolute.

The five men, on each side of the little bridge, are also arranged symmetrically: in two parallel lines, the intervals being the same in each group, and the two men on the right bank – whose backs alone are visible – placed in the centre of the intervals determined by their three companions on the left bank, who are facing the house, where A... appears behind the open window recess.

She is standing. In her hand she is holding a sheet of pale-blue paper of ordinary letter-paper size, which shows the creases where it has been folded into quarters. But her arm is half bent, and the sheet of paper is only at her waist; her eyes, which are looking far above it, wander towards the horizon, at the top of the opposite hillside. A... listens to the native chant, distant but still distinct, which reaches the veranda.

On the other side of the hallway door, under the symmetrical window of the office, Franck is sitting in his chair.

A..., who has gone to get the drinks herself, sets down the loaded tray on the coffee table. She uncorks the cognac and pours it into the three glasses lined up on the tray. Then she fills them with soda. Having distributed the first two, she sits down in her turn in the empty chair, holding the third glass in one hand.

This is when she asks if the usual ice cubes will be necessary, declaring that these bottles have come out of the refrigerator, though only one of the two has frosted over upon contact with the air.

She calls the boy. No one answers.

"One of us had better go," she says.

But neither she nor Franck moves.

In the pantry, the boy is already taking the ice cubes out of their trays, according to the orders his mistress gave him, he declares. And he adds that he is going to bring them right away, instead of specifying when this order is given.

On the veranda, Franck and A... have remained in their chairs. She has not been in any hurry about serving the ice: she has still not touched the shiny metal bucket which the boy has just set down next to her, its lustre already frosted over.

Like A... beside him, Franck looks straight ahead, towards the horizon at the top of the hillside opposite. A sheet of pale-blue paper, folded several times – probably in eighths – now sticks out of his right shirt pocket. The left pocket is still carefully buttoned, while the flap of the other one is now raised by the letter, which sticks above the edge of the khaki cloth by a good half-inch.

A... notices the pale-blue paper is attracting attention. She starts explaining about a misunderstanding between herself and the boy with regard to the ice. Then did she tell him not to bring it? In any case, this is the first time she has not succeeded in making herself understood by one of her servants.

"There has to be a first time for everything," she answers, with a calm smile. Her green eyes, which never blink, merely reflect the outline of a figure against the sky.

Down below, in the hollow of the valley, the arrangement of the workmen is no longer the same, at either end of the log bridge. Only one remains on the right bank, the other four being lined up opposite him. But their postures have not changed at all. Behind the single man, one of the new logs has disappeared: the one which was lying on top of two others. A log with earth-covered bark, however, has appeared on the left bank, quite a way behind the four workmen facing the house.

Franck stands up with sudden energy, and sets down on the coffee table the glass he has just emptied at one gulp. There is nothing left of the ice cube in the glass. Franck walks stiffly to the hallway door. He stops there. His head and the upper part of his body turn towards A..., who is still sitting in her chair.

"Forgive me, again, for being such a bad mechanic."

But A...'s face is not turned towards him, and the grimace which accompanies Franck's words has remained far outside her field of vision – a grimace that is, moreover, immediately absorbed, at the same time as the wrinkled white suit, by the shadow of the hallway.

At the bottom of the glass he has set down on the table as he left, a tiny piece of ice is melting, rounded on one side, on the other formed into a bevelled edge. A little further away come the bottle of soda, the cognacs, then the bridge crossing the little stream where the five crouching men are now arranged as follows: one on the right bank, two on the left, two others on the bridge itself, near its far end, all facing the same central point, which they seem to be considering with the closest attention.

There remain only two more new logs to put in place.

Then Franck and his hostess are sitting in the same chairs, but they have exchanged places: A... is in Franck's chair and vice versa. So now it is Franck who is nearest the coffee table where the ice bucket and the bottles are.

A... calls the boy.

He appears at once on the veranda, at the corner of the house. He walks with mechanical steps towards the little table, picks it up without spilling anything on it, sets the whole thing down a little further away, near his mistress. He then continues on his way without saying a word, in the same direction, with the same mechanical gait, towards the other corner of the house and the eastern side of the veranda, where he disappears.

Franck and A..., still silent and motionless in their chairs, continue to stare at the horizon.

Franck tells a story about his car's engine trouble, laughing and gesturing with a disproportionate energy and enthusiasm. He picks up his glass from the table beside him and empties it in one gulp, as if he had no need to open his throat to swallow the liquid: everything runs down into his stomach at once. He sets the glass down on the table, between his plate and the place mat. He begins eating again right away. His considerable appetite is made even more noticeable by the numerous, emphatic movements he makes: his right hand that picks up in turn the knife, the fork and the bread, the fork that passes alternately from the right hand to the left, the knife that cuts up the pieces of meat one by one and which is laid on the table after each use, so as to leave the fork free play as it changes hands, the comings and goings of the fork between plate and mouth, the rhythmic distortions of all the muscles of the face during a conscientious mastication which, even before being completed, is already accompanied by an accelerated repetition of the whole series.

The right hand picks up the bread and raises it to the mouth, the right hand sets the bread down on the white cloth and picks up the knife, the left hand picks up the fork, the fork sinks into the meat, the knife cuts off a piece of meat, the right hand sets down the knife on the cloth, the left hand puts the fork in the right hand, which sinks the fork into the piece of meat, which approaches the mouth, which begins to chew with movements of contraction and extension which are reflected all over the face, in the cheekbones, the eyes, the ears, while the right hand again picks up the fork and puts it in the left hand, then picks up the bread, then the knife, then the fork...

The boy comes in through the open pantry door. He approaches the table. His steps are increasingly jerky, as are

his gestures when he raises the plates one by
them on the sideboard and replace them by clea[
goes out immediately afterwards, moving arms and legs in
cadence, like a crude mechanism.

This is the moment when the scene of the squashing of
the centipede on the bare wall occurs: Franck stands up,
picks up his napkin, approaches the wall, squashes the
centipede against the wall, lifts his napkin, squashes the
centipede on the floor.

The hand with tapering fingers has clenched into a fist on
the white cloth. The five wide-spaced fingers have closed
over the palm with such force that they have pulled the
cloth with them. The cloth shows five convergent creases,
much longer than the fingers which have produced them.

Only the first joint is still visible. On the ring finger
gleams a thin ribbon of gold that barely rises above the
flesh. Around the hand radiate the creases, looser and
looser as they move out from the centre, but also wider and
wider, finally becoming a uniform white surface on which
Franck's brown, muscular hand, wearing a large flat ring of
the same type, comes to rest.

Just beside it, the knife blade has left on the cloth a tiny,
dark, elongated, sinuous stain surrounded by more tenuous
marks. The brown hand, after wavering in the vicinity a
moment, suddenly rises to the shirt pocket where it again
tries, with a mechanical movement, to push down the pale-
blue folded letter which sticks out by a good half-inch.

The shirt is made of a stiff fabric, a twilled cotton whose
khaki colour has faded slightly after many washings. Under
the upper edge of the pocket runs a line of horizontal
stitching over a sewn brace with the point downwards. At
the tip of this point is sewn the button normally intended to

close the pocket. The button is made of a yellowish plastic material; the thread that attaches it forms a little cross at the centre. The letter above is covered with a fine, close-set handwriting, perpendicular to the edge of the pocket.

To the right come, in order, the short sleeve of the khaki shirt, the bulging native terracotta pitcher which marks the middle of the sideboard, then, at the end of the latter, the two kerosene lamps, extinguished and set side by side against the wall; still further to the right, the corner of the room, immediately followed by the open leaf of the first window.

And Franck's car appears, brought into view through the window quite naturally by the conversation. It is a big blue sedan of American manufacture, whose body – though dusty – seems new. The motor too is in good condition: it never gives its owner any trouble.

The latter is still behind the wheel. Only his passenger has stepped out on the gravel of the courtyard. She is wearing shoes with extremely high heels and must be careful to put her feet down in places that are level. But she is not at all awkward at this exercise, the difficulty of which she does not even seem to notice. She stands motionless next to the front door of the car, leaning towards the grey imitation-leather upholstery, above the window which has been rolled down as far as it will go.

The white dress with the wide skirt almost disappears above the waist: the head, arms and upper part of the body, filling the window opening, also obscure what is happening inside. A... is probably gathering up the purchases she has just made to carry them with her. But the left elbow reappears, soon followed by the forearm, the wrist, the hand, which holds on to the edge of the window frame.

After another pause, the shoulders emerge into daylight too, then the neck, and the head with its heavy mass of black hair, whose loose curls are a little disarranged, and finally the right hand which holds by its string only an extremely tiny green cubical package.

Leaving the print of four parallel tapering fingers on the dusty enamel of the window frame, the left hand hurriedly arranges the hair, while A... walks away from the blue car and, after a last look back, heads towards the door with her decisive gait. The uneven surface of the courtyard seems to level out in front of her, for A... never even glances at her feet.

Then she is standing in front of the door which she has closed behind her. From this point she sees the whole house down the middle: the main room (living room on the left and dining room on the right, where the table is already set for dinner), the central hallway (off which open five doors, all closed, three on the right and two on the left), the veranda, and beyond its openwork balustrade, the opposite slope of the valley.

Starting from the crest, the slope is divided horizontally into three parts: an irregular strip of brush and two cultivated patches of different ages. The brush is reddish-coloured, dotted here and there with green brushes. A clump of trees marks the highest point of cultivation in this sector; it occupies the corner of a rectangular patch where the bare earth can still be distinguished in spots between the clusters of young leaves. Lower down, the second patch, in the shape of a trapezoid, is being harvested: the plate-sized white discs of the cut trunks are about as numerous as the adult trees still standing.

One side of this trapezoid is formed by the dirt road which ends at the little bridge over the stream. The five men are now arranged in a quincunx, two on each bank and one in the middle of the bridge, all facing upstream and watching the muddy water flowing between two vertical banks which have collapsed a little here and there.

On the right bank there still remain two new logs to be set in place. They form a kind of loose V with an open point across the road which rises towards the house and the garden.

A... is just coming home. She has been visiting Christiane, who has been kept from going out for several days by her child's poor health, as delicate as her mother's and just as badly adapted to colonial life. A..., whom Franck has driven home in his car, crosses the living room and walks down the hallway to her bedroom, which opens onto the terrace.

The bedroom windows have remained wide open all morning long. A... approaches the first one and closes its right-hand leaf, while the hand resting on the left one interrupts her gesture. The face turns in profile towards the half-opening, the neck straight, the ear cocked.

The low voice of the second driver reaches her.

The man is singing a native tune, a wordless, seemingly endless phrase which suddenly stops for no apparent reason. A..., finishing her gesture, closes the second leaf of the window.

Then she closes the two other windows. But she lowers none of the blinds.

She sits down in front of the dressing table and looks at herself in the oval mirror, motionless, her elbows on the marble top and her hands pressing on each side of her face against the temples. Not one of her features moves, nor the long-lashed eyelids, nor even the pupils at the centre of the green irises. Petrified by her own gaze, attentive and serene, she seems not to feel time passing.

Leaning to one side, her tortoiseshell comb in her hand, she rearranges her hair before coming to the dinner table. A mass of the heavy black curls hangs over the nape of her neck. The free hand plunges its tapering fingers into it.

A… is lying fully dressed on the bed. One of her legs rests on the satin spread; the other, bent at the knee, hangs half over the edge. The arm on this side is bent towards the head lying on the bolster. Stretched across the wide bed, the other arm lies out from the body at approximately a forty-five-degree angle. Her face is turned upwards towards the ceiling. Her eyes are made still larger by the darkness.

Near the bed, against the same wall, is the heavy chest. A… is standing in front of the open top drawer, on which she is leaning in order to look for something, or else to arrange the contents. The operation takes a long time and requires no movement of the body.

She is sitting in the chair between the hallway door and the writing table. She is rereading a letter which shows the creases where it has been folded. Her long legs are crossed. Her right hand is holding the sheet in front of her face; her left hand is gripping the end of the armrest.

A… is writing, sitting at the table near the first window. Actually, she is getting ready to write, unless she has just finished her letter. The pen remains suspended an inch or so above the paper. Her face is raised towards the calendar hanging on the wall.

Between this first window and the second, there is just room enough for the large wardrobe. A…, who is standing beside it, is therefore visible only from the third window, the one that overlooks the west gable end. It is a mirrored wardrobe. A… is carefully examining her face at close range.

Now she has moved still further to the right, into the corner of the room which also constitutes the south-west corner of the house. It would be easy to observe her from one of the two doors, that of the hallway or that of the bathroom, but the doors are of wood, without blinds that can be seen through. As for the blinds on the three windows, none of them are now arranged so that anything can be seen through them.

Now the house is empty

A… has gone to town with Franck to make a few necessary purchases. She has not said what they were.

They left very early, so as to have enough time to run their errands and still be able to return to the plantation the same night.

Having left the house at six thirty this morning, they expect to be back a little after midnight, which means an absence of eighteen hours, at least eight of which will be spent on the road, if all goes well.

But delays are always likely on these bad roads. Even if they start back at the expected time, immediately after a quick dinner, the travellers might not get home until around one in the morning, or even much later.

Meanwhile the house is empty. All the windows of the bedroom are open, as well as its two doors, opening onto the hallway and the bathroom. The door between the bathroom and the hallway is also wide open, as is that from the hallway to the central part of the veranda.

The veranda is empty too; none of the armchairs have been brought outside this morning, nor has the table that is used for cocktails and coffee. But under the open office window, the flagstones show the trace of eight chair legs: two sets of four shiny points, smoother than the stone around them. The two left-hand corners of the right-hand square are scarcely two inches away from the two right-hand corners of the left-hand square.

These shiny points are clearly visible only from the balustrade. They disappear when the observer comes closer. Looking down from the window immediately above them, it becomes impossible to tell where they are.

The furnishings of this room are very simple: files and shelves against the walls, two chairs, the massive desk. On one corner of the latter stands a little mother-of-pearl-inlaid frame with a photograph taken at the seaside in Europe. A... is sitting on the terrace of a large café. Her chair is set at an angle to the table on which she is about to set down her glass.

The table is a metal disc pierced with innumerable holes, the largest of which form a complicated rosette: a series of S's all starting at the centre, like double-curved spokes of a wheel, and each spiralling at the other end, at the periphery of the disc.

The base supporting the table consists of a slender triple stem whose strands separate to converge again, coiling (in three vertical planes through the axis of the system) into three similar volutes, whose lower whorls rest on the ground and are bound together by a ring placed a little higher on the curve.

The chair is similarly constructed, with perforated metal sheets and stems. It is harder to follow its convolutions, because of the person sitting on it, who largely conceals them from view.

On the table near a second glass, at the right edge of the picture, are a man's hand and the cuff of a jacket sleeve, cut off by the white vertical margin.

All the other portions of chairs evident in the photograph seem to belong to unoccupied seats. There is no one on the veranda, as elsewhere in the house.

In the dining room, a single place has been set for lunch, on the side of the table facing the pantry door and the long, low sideboard extending from this door to the window.

The window is closed. The courtyard is empty. The second driver must have parked the truck near the sheds, to wash it. In the place it usually occupies, all that remains is a large black spot contrasting with the dusty surface of the courtyard. This is a little oil which has dripped out of the motor, always in the same place.

It is easy to make this spot disappear, thanks to the flaws in the rough glass of the window: the blackened surface has merely to be brought into proximity with one of the flaws of the window pane by successive experiments.

The spot begins growing larger, one of its sides bulging to form a rounded protuberance itself larger than the initial object. But a few fractions of an inch further, this bulge is transformed into a series of tiny concentric crescents which diminish until they are only lines, while the other side of the spot shrinks, leaving behind it a stalk-shaped appendage which bulges in its turn for a second; then suddenly everything disappears.

Behind the glass now, in the angle determined by the central vertical frame and the horizontal crosspiece, there

is only the greyish-beige colour of the dusty gra
constitutes the surface of the courtyard.

On the opposite wall, the centipede is there, in its tel\
spot, right in the middle of the panel.

It has stopped, a tiny oblique line two inches long at eye
level, halfway between the skirting board (at the hall doorway) and the corner of the ceiling. The creature is motionless. Only its antennae rise and fall one after the other in an
alternating, slow, but continuous movement.

At its posterior extremity, the considerable development
of the legs – of the last pair especially, which are longer than
the antennae – identifies it unquestionably as the *Scutigera*,
also known as the "spider centipede" or "minute centipede".
So called because of a native belief as to the rapidity of the
action of its bite – supposedly deadly. Actually this species
is not very venomous; it is much less so, in any case, than
many *Scolopendra* common in the region.

Suddenly the anterior part of the body begins to move,
executing a rotation which curves the dark line towards the
lower part of the wall. And immediately, without having
time to go any further, the creature falls onto the tiles, still
twisting and curling up its long legs while its mandibles
rapidly open and close around its mouth in a quivering
reflex.

Ten seconds later, it is nothing more than a reddish pulp
in which are mingled the debris of unrecognized sections.

But on the bare wall, on the contrary, the image of the
squashed *Scutigera* is perfectly clear, incomplete but not
blurred, reproduced with the faithfulness of an anatomical
drawing in which only a portion of the elements are shown:
an antenna, two curving mandibles, the head and the first
joint, half of the second, a few large legs, etc…

The outline seems indelible. It has no relief, none of the thickness of a dried stain which would come off if scratched at with a fingernail. It looks more like brown ink impregnating the surface layer of the paint.

Besides, it is not practical to wash the wall. This dull-finish paint is much more fragile than the ordinary gloss paint with linseed oil in it which was previously used on the walls of this room. The best solution would be to use an eraser, a hard, fine-grained eraser which would gradually wear down the soiled surface – the typewriter eraser, for instance, which is in the top-left desk drawer.

The slender traces of bits of legs or antennae come off right away, with the first strokes of the eraser. The larger part of the body, already quite pale, is curved into a question mark that becomes increasingly vague towards the tip of the curve, and soon disappears completely. But the head and the first joints require a more extensive rubbing: after losing its colour, the remaining shape stays the same for quite a long time. The outlines have become only a little less sharp. The hard eraser passing back and forth over the same point does not have much effect now.

A complementary operation seems in order: to scratch the surface very lightly with the corner of a razor blade. Some white dust rises from the wall. The precision of the tool permits the area exposed to its effect to be carefully determined. A new rubbing with the eraser now finishes off the work quite easily.

The stain has disappeared altogether. There now remains only a vaguely outlined paler area, without any apparent depression on the surface, which might pass for an insignificant defect in the finish at worst.

The paper is much thinner nevertheless; it more translucid, uneven, a little downy. The same blade, bent between two fingers to raise the centre of its cutting edge, also serves to shave off the fluff the eraser has made. The back of a fingernail finally smoothes down the last roughness.

In broad daylight, a closer inspection of the pale-blue sheet reveals that two short pen strokes have resisted everything, doubtless because they were made too heavily. Unless a new word, skilfully arranged to cover up these two unnecessary strokes, replaces the old one on the page, the traces of black ink will still be visible there. Unless the eraser is used once again.

It stands out clearly against the dark wood of the desk, as does the razor blade, and the foot of the mother-of-pearl-inlaid frame where A… is about to set down her glass on the round table with its many perforations. The eraser is a thin pink disc whose central part is covered by a little tin-plate circle. The razor blade is a flat, polished rectangle, its short sides rounded, and pierced with three holes in a line. The central hole is circular; the two others, one on each side, reproduce precisely, on a much smaller scale, the general shape of the blade – that is, a rectangle with its short sides rounded.

Instead of looking at the glass she is about to set down, A…, whose chair is set at an angle to the table, is turning in the opposite direction to smile at the photographer, as if encouraging him to take this candid shot.

The photographer has not lowered his camera to put it on a level with his model. In fact he seems to have climbed up onto something: a stone bench, a step or a low wall. A… has to raise her head to turn her face towards the lens. The slender neck is erect, turned towards the right. On this side, the hand is resting easily on the far edge of the chair, against the thigh, the bare arm slightly bent at the elbow. The knees are apart, the legs half extended, ankles crossed.

The delicate waist is encircled by a wide belt with a triple clasp. The left arm, extended, holds the glass a few inches above the openwork table.

The lustrous black curls fall free to the shoulders. The flood of heavy locks with reddish highlights trembles at the slightest movement the head makes. The head must be shaken with tiny movements, imperceptible in themselves, but amplified by the mass of hair, creating gleaming, quickly vanishing eddies whose sudden intensity is reawakened in unlooked-for convulsions a little lower... lower still... and a last spasm much lower.

The face, hidden because of her position, is bending over the table where the invisible hands are busy with some long-drawn-out and laborious task: mending a stocking, polishing nails, a tiny pencil drawing, erasing a stain or a badly chosen word. From time to time she straightens up and leans back to judge her work from a distance. With a slow gesture, she pushes back a shorter strand of hair which has come loose from this unstable arrangement and is annoying her.

But the rebellious curl remains on the white silk of her shoulder, where it traces a wavy line ending in a hook. Under the moving mass of hair, the delicate waist is divided vertically, along the spine, by the narrow line of the metal zipper.

A... is standing on the veranda, at the corner of the house, near the square column that supports the south-west corner of the roof. She is leaning both hands on the railing, facing south, looking over the garden and the whole valley.

She is in full sunlight. The sun strikes her directly on the forehead. But she does not mind it, even at noon. Her foreshortened shadow falls perpendicularly across the flagstones, of which it covers lengthwise no more than one. A quarter of an inch behind it begins the roof's shadow, parallel with the railing. The sun is almost at its zenith.

The two extended arms are an equal distance from either side of the hips. The hands are both holding the wooden handrail in the same way. Since A... is standing with half her weight on each of her high-heeled shoes, the symmetry of her whole body is perfect.

A... is standing in front of one of the closed windows of the living room, directly opposite the dirt road that comes down from the highway. Through the glass she looks straight ahead of her, towards the place where the road enters the dusty courtyard, which the shadow of the house darkens with a strip about three yards wide. The rest of the courtyard is white in the sunlight.

The large room, in comparison, seems dark. Her dress takes on a cold blue tinge from the shadows. A... does not move. She continues to stare at the courtyard and the road between the banana trees, straight ahead of her.

A... is in the bathroom, whose door to the hallway she has left ajar. She is not washing. She is standing against the white lacquer table in front of the square window that comes down to her breast. Beyond the open window recess, above the veranda, the openwork balustrade, the garden down the slope, her eyes can see only the green mass of the banana trees and, further on, passing above the highway going down to the plain, the rocky spur of the plateau, behind which the sun has just disappeared.

71

The night does not take long to fall in these countries without twilight. The lacquered table suddenly turns deep blue, like her dress, the white floor and the sides of the bathtub. The whole room is plunged into darkness.

Only the square of the window makes a spot of paler violet, against which A...'s black silhouette appears: the line of her shoulders and arms, the contour of her hair. It is impossible, in this light, to know if her head is turned towards the window or in the opposite direction.

In the office, the light suddenly fades. The sun has set. A... can no longer be seen. The photograph can be distinguished only by the mother-of-pearl edges of its frame, which gleam in the remaining light. In front of it shines the oblong of the razor blade and the metal ellipse in the centre of the eraser. But this lasts only a moment. Now the eye can distinguish nothing any longer, despite the open windows.

The five workmen are still at their post, in the hollow of the valley, squatting in a quincunx on the little bridge. The running water of the stream still glitters in the last reflections of the daylight. And then nothing more.

On the veranda, A... will have to close her book soon. She has continued reading until the light has become too faint. Then she lifts her face, puts the book down on the coffee table within arm's reach, and remains motionless, her bare arms stretched out on the elbow rests, leaning back in her chair, her eyes wide open, staring at the empty sky, the absent banana trees, the railing engulfed in its turn by the darkness.

And the deafening racket of the crickets already fills the night, as if it had never ceased to be there. The continuous grating, without progression or nuance, immediately reaches its full development, has been at its climax for some time already, minutes or hours, for no beginning can be perceived at any one moment.

Now the area is altogether dark. Although there is time for eyes to become accustomed to it, no object appears, even those closest.

But now once again there are balusters towards the corner of the house – half-balusters, more precisely – and a handrail on top, and the flagstones gradually appear at their feet. The corner of the wall reveals its vertical line. A warm glow appears behind it.

It is a lit lamp, one of the big kerosene lamps that reveals two walking legs as far up as the bare knees and calves. The boy approaches, holding the lamp at arm's length. Shadows dance in all directions.

The boy has not yet reached the little table when A...'s voice can be heard, precise and low; she tells him to put the lamp in the dining room, after being careful to shut the windows, as every evening.

"You know you're not supposed to bring the lamp out here. It attracts mosquitoes."

The boy has said nothing and has not stopped for even a moment. Even the regularity of his gait has not been altered. Having reached a point opposite the door, he makes a quarter-turn towards the hallway, where he disappears, leaving behind him only a flaming gleam: the doorway, a rectangle on the veranda flagstones, and six balusters at the other end. Then nothing more.

A... has not turned her head in speaking to the boy. Her face has received the lamp's beams on the right side. This brightly illuminated profile still clings to the retina. In the darkness where no object can be seen, even those closest, the luminous spot shifts at will, without its intensity fading, keeping the outline of the forehead, the nose, the chin, the mouth...

The spot is on the wall of the house, on the flagstones, against the empty sky. It is everywhere in the valley, from the garden to the stream and up the opposite slope. It is in the office too, in the bedroom, in the dining room, in the living room, in the courtyard, on the road up to the highway.

But A... has not moved an inch. She has not opened her mouth to speak, her voice has not interrupted the racket of the nocturnal crickets; the boy has not come out on the veranda, so he has not brought the lamp, knowing perfectly well that his mistress does not want it.

He has carried it into her bedroom, where his mistress is now preparing to leave.

The lamp is set on the dressing table. A... is putting on the last of her discreet make-up: the lipstick which merely accentuates the natural colour of her lips, but which seems darker in this glaring light.

Dawn has not yet broken.

Franck will come soon to call for A... and take her down to the port. She is sitting in front of the oval mirror, where her full face is reflected, lit from only one side, at a short distance from her own face seen in profile.

A... bends towards the mirror. The two faces come closer. They are no more than four inches from each other, but they keep their forms and their respective positions: a profile and a full face, parallel to each other.

The right hand and the hand in the mirror trace on the lips and on their reflection the exact image of the lips, somewhat brighter, clearer, slightly darker.

Two light knocks sound at the hallway door.

The bright lips and the lips in profile move in perfect synchronization:

"Yes, what is it?"

The voice is restrained, as in a sickroom, or like the voice of a thief talking to his accomplice.

"The gentleman, he is here," the boy's voice answers on the other side of the door.

No sound of a motor, however, has broken the silence (which was no silence, but the continuous hissing of the kerosene lamp).

A... says: "I'm coming."

She calmly finishes the curving rim above her chin with an assured gesture.

She stands up, crosses the room, walks around the big bed, picks up her handbag on the chest and the white wide-brimmed straw hat. She opens the door without making any noise (though without excessive precautions), goes out, closes the door behind her.

The sound of her steps fades down the hallway.

The entrance door opens and closes.

It is six thirty.

The whole house is empty. It has been empty since morning.

It is now six thirty. The sun has disappeared behind the rocky spur which bounds the main section of the plateau.

The night is black and heavy, without the least breath of air, full of the deafening noise of crickets, which seems to have been going on for ever.

A... is not returning for dinner, which she will take in town with Franck before starting back. She has said nothing about preparing anything for her return. Because she will

75

hing. It is useless to expect her. In any case, it
xpect her at dinner.

hing-room table the boy has set a single place,
on e long, low sideboard which takes up almost the
entire wall between the open pantry door and the closed
window overlooking the courtyard. The curtains, which
have not been drawn, reveal the six black panes of the
window.

A single lamp illuminates the large room. It is placed on the
south-west corner of the table (that is, towards the pantry),
lighting up the white cloth. To the right of the lamp, a little
spot of sauce marks Franck's place: an elongated, sinuous
stain surrounded by more tenuous markings. On the other
side, the lamp's beams strike perpendicularly against the
nearby bare wall, showing quite clearly in the full light the
image of the centipede Franck squashed.

If each of the *Scutigera*'s legs consists of four joints of
varying lengths, none of those which are outlined here, on
the full finish of the paint, are intact – except perhaps one,
the first on the left. But it is stretched out, almost straight, so
that its joints are not easy to determine with any certitude.
The original leg may have been considerably longer. The
antenna, too, has doubtless not been printed on the wall to
its very tip.

On the white plate, a land crab spreads out its five pairs
of clearly jointed, muscular legs. Around its mouth, many
smaller appendages are arranged in pairs. The creature uses
them to produce a kind of crackling sound, audible at close
range, like that which the *Scutigera* makes in certain cases.

But the lamp prevents any such sound from being heard
because of its constant hissing, of which the ear is aware
only when it tries to hear any other sound.

On the veranda, where the boy has now carried the little table and one of the low chairs, the sound of the lamp fades whenever an animal cry interrupts it.

The crickets have fallen silent for some time now. The night is already well advanced. There is neither moon nor stars. There is not a breath of air. It is a black, calm, hot night, like all the rest, occasionally interrupted only by the short, shrill calls of tiny nocturnal carnivores, the sudden buzzing of a beetle, the rustle of a bat's wing.

Then a silence. But a fainter sound, something like a hum, makes the ear strain... It stops at once. And the lamp's hissing can be heard.

Besides, it was more like a growl than the sound of a car motor. A... has not yet returned. They are a little late, which is quite normal on these bad roads.

There is no doubt the lamp draws mosquitoes, but it draws them towards its own light. So it is enough to put it at some distance in order not to be bothered by them or by other insects.

They all turn round the glass, accompanying the even hiss of the kerosene lamp with their circular flights. Their small size, their relative distance, their speed – all the greater the closer they fly to the source of light – keep the shape of the bodies and wings from being recognized. It is not even possible to distinguish among the different species, not to mention naming them. They are merely particles in motion, describing more or less flattened ellipses in horizontal planes or at slight angles, cutting the elongated cylinder of the lamp at various levels.

But the orbits are rarely centred on the lamp; almost all fly further to one side, right or left, than the other – so far, sometimes, that the tiny body disappears in the darkness.

It immediately returns to view – or another returns in its place – and soon retraces its orbit, so that it circles with others of its kind in a common, harshly illuminated zone about a yard and a half long.

At every moment, certain ellipses narrow until they become tangent to the lamp on each side (front and back). They are then reduced to their smallest dimensions in both directions, and attain their highest speeds. But they do not maintain this accelerated rhythm long: by a sudden withdrawal, the generating element resumes a calmer gravitation.

Besides, whether it is a question of amplitude, shape or the more or less eccentric situation, the variations are probably incessant within the swarm. To follow them it would be necessary to differentiate individuals. Since this is impossible, a certain general unity is established within which the local crises, arrivals, departures and permutations no longer enter into account.

Shrill and short, an animal's cry sounds quite close, seeming to come from the garden, just at the foot of the veranda. Then the same cry, after three seconds, indicates its presence on the other side of the house. And again there is silence, which is not silence but a succession of identical, shriller, more remote cries in the mass of the banana trees near the stream, perhaps on the opposite slope, reaching from one end of the valley to the other.

Now there is a duller sound, less fugitive, that attracts the attention: a kind of growl, or rumble, or hum...

But even before being sufficiently clear to be identified, the noise stops. The ear, which vainly tries to locate it again in the darkness, no longer hears anything in its place except the hiss of the kerosene lamp.

Its sound is plaintive, high-pitched, somewhat nasal. But its complexity permits it to have overtones at various levels. Of an absolute evenness, both muffled and shrill, it fills the night and the ears as if it came from nowhere.

Around the lamp, the circling of the insects is still the same. By examining it closely, however, the eye at last manages to make out some bodies that are larger than others. Yet this is not enough to determine their nature. Against the black background they form only bright points which become increasingly brilliant as they approach the light, turning black as soon as they pass in front of the lamp with the light behind them, then recovering all their brilliance, the intensity of which now decreases towards the tip of the orbit.

In the suddenness of its return towards the glass, the bright point violently plunges against it, producing a dry click. Fallen on the table, it has become a tiny reddish beetle with closed wing cases, which slowly circles on the darker wood.

Other creatures similar to this one have already fallen on the table; they wander there, tracing uncertain paths with many detours and problematical objectives. Suddenly raising its wing cases into a V with curved sides, one of them extends its filmy wings, takes off, and immediately returns to the swarm of flying bodies.

But it constitutes one of the swarm's heaviest, slowest elements, therefore less difficult for the eyes to follow. The whorls which it describes are also probably among the more capricious: they include loops, garlands, sudden ascents and brutal falls, changes of direction, abrupt retracings...

The duller sound has already lasted several seconds, or even several minutes now: a kind of growling, or rumble or hum of a motor, the motor of an automobile on the highway rising towards the plateau. It fades for a moment, only to resume all the more clearly. This time it certainly is the sound of a car on the road.

It rises in pitch as it draws nearer. It fills the whole valley with its regular, monotonous throbbing, much louder than it seems in daylight. Its importance quickly surpasses what would normally be expected of a mere sedan.

The sun has now reached the point where the dirt road turns off the highway towards the plantation. Instead of slowing down to turn to the right, it continues its uniform progress, now reaching the ears from behind the house, towards the east gable end. It has gone past the turn-off.

Having reached the flat section of the road, just below the rocky rim where the plateau comes to an end, the truck shifts gears and continues with a fainter rumble. The sound gradually fades away, as the truck drives east, its powerful headlights lighting up the clumps of stiff-leaved trees that dot the brush on the way to the next plantation – Franck's.

His car might have had engine trouble again. They should have been back long since.

Around the kerosene lamps the ellipses continue to turn, lengthening, shortening, moving off to the right or left, rising, falling or swaying first to one side then to the other, mingling in an increasingly tangled skein in which no autonomous curve remains identifiable.

A... should have been back long since.

Nevertheless there is no lack of probable reasons for the delay. Apart from an accident – never impossible – there are the two successive punctures that oblige the driver to repair one of the tyres himself: take off the wheel, remove the inner tube, find the hole in the light from the headlights, etc...; there is a severance of some electrical connection, due to a jolt that was too violent, which might cut the headlight wires, involving long investigations and a haphazard mending job by the poor light of a pocket torch. The road is in such bad condition that an important part of the car's engine might be damaged, if the car is going too fast: shock-absorber broken, axle bent, crankcase split... There is also the help that cannot be refused to another driver in difficulty. There are the various risks delaying the departure itself: unforeseen prolongation of some errand, excessive slowness of the waiter, invitation to dinner accepted at the last minute with a friend met by chance, etc., etc... There is, last of all, the driver's fatigue which has made him postpone his return to the next day.

The sound of a truck coming up the road along the near slope of the valley fills the air again. It is moving east from one end of the field of hearing to the other, reaching its maximum volume as it passes behind the house. It is moving just as fast as the preceding one, which for a moment might cause it to be confused with a touring car, but the sound is much too loud. The truck is apparently empty. They are the banana trucks returning, empty, from the port, after leaving their stems in the sheds on the docks, where the *Cap Saint-Jean* is moored.

This is the picture on the post-office calendar hanging on the bedroom wall. The brand-new white ship is moored beside the long pier which juts out into the sea from the lower margin. The structure of the pier cannot be clearly discerned: apparently there is a wood (or iron) framework supporting a tar-paved roadway. While the pier is virtually at water level, the ship's sides rise far above it. The ship is shown head on, revealing the vertical line of its stem and its two smooth sides, of which only one is in sunlight.

The ship and the pier take up the centre of the picture, the former to the left, the latter on the right. Around it, the sea is covered with canoes and rowing boats: eight are clearly visible and three others suggested in the background. A less fragile craft, provided with a square wind-filled sail, is about to pass the end of the pier. The latter is covered with a brightly dressed crowd near a pile of bales in front of the ship.

A little to one side, but in the foreground, turning his back to this confusion and to the great white ship provoking it, someone in European clothes is looking towards the right side of the picture at some sort of flotsam, the vague mass of which is floating a few yards away from him. The surface of the water is faintly rippled with a short, regular swell, which advances towards the man. The flotsam, half-raised by the tide, seems to be an old piece of clothing or an empty sack.

The largest of the canoes is quite near it, but is moving away from it; all the attention of the two natives manoeuvring it is occupied by the concussion of a little wave against the prow, falling back in a plume of foam caught in mid-air by the camera.

To the left of the pier, the sea is calmer. It is also a deeper green. Large patches of oil form blue-green stains at the foot of the pier. It is on this side that the *Cap Saint-Jean* is moored; towards it converges the interest of all the other people comprising the scene. Because of the position the ship occupies, its superstructures are somewhat vague, save for the forecastle, the bridge, the top of the smokestack and the first loading mast with its oblique arm, pullies, cables and ropes.

At the top of the mast a bird is perched, not a sea bird but a vulture with a bare neck. A second such bird soars in the sky, above and to the right; its wings are stretched straight across, widespread and strongly raked towards the top of the mast; the bird is executing a banked turn. Still higher runs a horizontal white margin half an inch wide, then a red border narrower by half.

Above the calendar, which is hanging from a drawing pin by a red thread in the shape of a circumflex accent, the wooden wall is painted pale grey. Other pin holes show nearby. A larger hole to the left marks the location of a missing screw or of a heavy nail.

Aside from these perforations, the paint in the bedroom is in good condition. The four walls, like those of the whole house, are covered with vertical laths two inches wide separated by a double groove. The depth of these grooves shows a deep shadow under the glare of the kerosene lamp.

This striped effect is reproduced on all four sides of the square bedroom – actually cubical, since it is as high as it is wide or long. The ceiling, moreover, is also covered by the same grey laths. As for the floor, it too is similarly constructed, as is evidenced by the clearly marked longitudinal interstices, hollowed out by the frequent wash-ings that discolour the wood laths, and parallel to the grooves of the ceiling.

Thus the six interior surfaces of the cube are distinctly outlined by thin laths of constant dimensions, vertical on the four vertical surfaces, running east and west on the two horizontal surfaces. When the lamp sways a little at the end of an extended arm, all these lines, with their short, moving shadows, seem animated with a general swirling movement.

The outside walls of the house are made of planks set horizontally; they are also wider – about eight inches –

and overlap each other on the outer edge. Their surface is therefore not contained within a single vertical plane, but in many parallel planes, inclined at several degrees' pitch and a plank's thickness from each other.

The windows are framed by a moulding and topped by a pediment in the shape of a flattened triangle. The laths which compose these embellishments have been nailed above the imbricated boards constituting the walls, so that the two systems are in contact only at a series of ridges (the inner edge of each board), between which exist considerable gaps.

Only the two horizontal mouldings are fastened along their entire surface: the base of the pediment and the base of the frame beneath the window. From one corner of the window, a dark liquid has flowed down over the wood, crossing the boards one after another from ridge to ridge, then the concrete substructure, making an increasingly narrow streak which finally dwindles to a line, and reaches the veranda floor in the middle of a flagstone, ending there in a little round spot.

The nearby flagstones are perfectly clean. They are frequently washed – as recently as this afternoon. The smooth stone has a dull, greyish surface, oily to the touch. The stones are large; starting from the round spot, following the wall, there are only five and a half until the doorstep into the hallway.

The door is also framed by a wooden moulding and topped by a flattened triangle pediment. On the other side of the sill, the floor consists of tiles much smaller than the flagstones, half their size in each direction. Instead of being smooth like the veranda flagstones, they are criss-crossed in one or the other diagonal direction by shallow grooves; the grooved areas are as wide as the ribs – that is, a few fractions of an inch. Their arrangement alternates from one tile to the next, so that the floor is set in successive chevrons. This low relief, scarcely visible in daylight, is accentuated by artificial light, especially at a certain distance ahead of the lamp, and still more if the latter is set on the floor.

The slight swaying of the lamp advancing along the hall-way animates the uninterrupted series of chevrons with a continual undulation like that of waves.

The same tiling continues, without any separation, in the living room/dining room. The area where the table and chairs are located is covered with a fibre carpet; the shadow of their legs swirls quickly across it, anticlockwise.

Behind the table, in the centre of the long sideboard, the native pitcher looks even larger: its bulging shape, made of unglazed red clay, casts a dense shadow which enlarges as the source of light draws nearer, a black disc surmounted by an isosceles trapezoid (whose base is at the top) and a thin curve which connects the circular side to one of the ends of the trapezoid.

The pantry door is closed. Between it and the doorway to the hall is the centipede. It is enormous: one of the largest to be found in this climate. With its long antennae and its huge legs spread on each side of its body, it covers the area of an ordinary dinner plate. The shadow of various appendages doubles their already considerable number on the light-coloured paint.

The body is curved towards the bottom: its front section is twisted towards the skirting board, while the last joints keep their original orientation – that of a straight line cutting diagonally across the panel from the hall doorway to the corner of the ceiling above the closed pantry door.

The creature is motionless, alert, as if sensing danger. Only its antennae are alternately raised and lowered in a swaying movement, slow but continuous.

Suddenly the front part of the body begins moving, executing a rotation which turns the creature towards the bottom of the wall. And immediately, without having a chance to go any further, the centipede falls on the tiles, half-twisted, and curling its long legs one after the other while its mandibles rapidly open and close in a reflex quiver... It is possible for an ear close enough to hear the faint crackling they produce.

The sound is that of the comb in the long hair. The tortoise-shell teeth pass again and again from top to bottom of the thick black mass with its reddish highlights, electrifying the tips and making the soft, freshly washed hair crackle during the entire descent of the delicate hand – the delicate hand with tapering fingers that gradually closes on the strands of hair.

The two long antennae accelerate their alternating swaying. The creature has stopped in the centre of the wall, at eye level. The considerable development of the posterior legs identifies it unmistakably as the *Scutigera* or "spider centipede". In the silence, from time to time, the characteristic buzzing can be heard, probably made by the buccal appendages.

Franck, without saying a word, stands up, wads his napkin into a ball as he cautiously approaches, and squashes the creature against the wall. Then, with his foot, he squashes it against the bedroom floor.

Then he comes back towards the bed and, in passing, hangs the towel on its metal rack near the washbasin.

The hand with the tapering fingers has clenched into a fist on the white sheet. The five widespread fingers have closed

over the palm with such force that they have drawn ...~
cloth with them: the latter shows five convergent creases...
But the mosquito netting falls back all around the bed,
interposing the opaque veil of its innumerable meshes,
where rectangular patches reinforce the torn places.

In his haste to reach his goal, Franck increases his speed.
The jolts become more violent. Nevertheless he continues
to drive faster. In the darkness, he has not seen the hole
running halfway across the road. The car makes a leap,
skids... On this bad road the driver cannot straighten out
in time. The blue sedan is going to crash into a roadside
tree, whose rigid foliage scarcely shivers under the impact,
despite its violence.

The car immediately bursts into flames. The whole brush
is illuminated by the crackling, spreading fire. It is the
sound the centipede makes, motionless again on the wall,
in the centre of the panel.

Listening to it more carefully, this sound is more like a
breath than a crackling: the brush is now moving down the
loosened hair. No sooner has it reached the bottom than it
quickly enters the ascending phase of the cycle, describing
a curve which brings it back to its point of departure on
the smooth hair of the head, where it begins moving down
once again.

On the opposite wall of the bedroom, the vulture is still
at the same point in its banked turn. A little below it, on
top of the ship's mast, the other bird has not moved either.
Below, in the foreground, the piece of cloth is still half
raised by the same undulation of the swell. And the two
natives in the canoe have not stopped looking at the plume
of foam still about to fall back on the prow of their fragile
craft.

And down below, the table top offers a varnished surface where the leather writing case is in its place, parallel with the long side of the table. To the left, a circle of felt intended for this use receives the circular base of the kerosene lamp.

Inside the writing case, the green blotter is covered with fragments of handwriting in black ink: tiny lines, arcs, crosses, loops, etc... no complete letter can be made out, even in a mirror. Eleven sheets of pale-blue writing paper of ordinary commercial size have been slipped into the side pocket of the portfolio. The first of these shows the evident traces of a word scratched out – on the upper right – of which only two tiny lines remain, greatly lightened by the eraser. The paper at this point is thinner, more translucent, but its grain is almost smooth, ready for the new inscription. As for the old letters, those which were there before, it is not possible to reconstitute them. The leather writing case contains nothing else.

In the drawer of the table, there are two pads of writing paper; one is new, the second is almost used up. The size of the sheets, their quality and their pale-blue colour are identical with those of the preceding ones. Beside them there lie three packets of envelopes lined with dark blue, still surrounded by their white band. But one of the packets is missing a good half of its envelopes, and the band is loose around those that remain.

Except for two black pencils, a circular typewriter eraser, the novel that has been the object of many discussions and an unused booklet of stamps, there is nothing else in the drawer.

The top drawer of the heavy chest requires a longer inventory. In its right half are several boxes full of old letters; almost all are still in their envelopes, with stamps from Europe or Africa: letters from A...'s family, letters from various friends.

A series of faint slaps is audible from the west side of the veranda, on the other side of the bed, behind the window with its lowered blinds. This might be the sound of steps on the flagstones. Yet the boy and the cook must long since be in bed. Besides, their feet – either bare or in espadrilles – are completely silent.

The noise has stopped again. If it was actually a step, it was a quick, slight, furtive one. It did not sound like a man's step, but that of a four-footed creature: some wild dog that managed to get up onto the veranda.

It has disappeared too quickly to leave a precise impression: the ear has not even had time to hear it. How many times was the faint impact repeated against the flagstones? Barely five or six, or even less. Not many for a passing dog. The fall of a big lizard from the eaves often produces a similar muddled "slap" – but then it would have taken five or six lizards falling one after another, which is unlikely... Only three lizards? That would be too many too. Perhaps, after all, the noise was repeated only twice.

As it fades in time, its likelihood diminishes. Now it is as if there had been nothing at all. Through the chinks of the blinds a little later, it is, of course, impossible to see anything at all. All that can be done is to close the blinds by manipulating the cord at the side.

The bedroom is closed again. The chevrons of the floor tiles, the grooves of the walls and those of the ceiling turn faster and faster. Standing on the pier, the person watching the floating debris begins to bend over, without losing any of his stiffness. He is wearing a well-cut white suit and has a colonial helmet on his head. The tips of his black moustache are waxed and point upwards in an old-fashioned style.

No. His face, which is not illuminated by the sun, lets nothing be surmised, not even the colour of his skin. It looks as if the little wave, continuing its advance, will unfold the piece of material and reveal whether it is an article of clothing, a canvas sack or something else, if there is still enough daylight to see.

At this moment the light suddenly goes out.

It has probably faded gradually, up to now, but this is not for sure. Was its range shortened? Was its colour yellower?

Yet the pump valve was primed several times early in the evening. Has all the kerosene been burnt already? Had the boy forgotten to fill the reservoir? Or does the suddenness of the phenomenon indicate the sudden obstruction of a tube, due to some impurity in the fuel?

In any case, relighting the lamp is too complicated to bother about. To cross the bedroom in darkness is not so difficult, nor to reach the big chest and its open drawer, the packages of unimportant letters, the boxes of buttons, the balls of yarn, a skein of fine silk threads like hair, nor to close the drawer again.

The absence of the hissing of the kerosene lamp makes it easier to understand the considerable volume it produced. The chain which was gradually unravelling has suddenly been broken or unhooked, abandoning the cubical cage to its own fate: falling free. The animals too must have fallen silent, one by one, in the valley. The silence is such that the faintest movements become impracticable.

Like this shapeless darkness, the silky hair flows between the curving fingers. It falls free, thickens, pushes its tentacles in all directions, coiling over itself in an increasingly complex skein, whose convolutions and apparent mazes continue to let the fingers pass through it with the same indifference, with the same ease.

With the same ease, the hair lets itself be unknotted, falls over the shoulder in a docile tide while the brush moves smoothly from top to bottom, from top to bottom, from top to bottom, guided now by the breathing alone, which in the complete darkness is enough to create a regular rhythm capable of measuring something, if something remains to measure, to limit, to describe in the total darkness, until the day breaks, now.

The day has broken long since. At the bottom of the two windows facing south, rays of light filter through the chinks of the closed blinds. For the sun to strike the façade at this angle, it must already be quite high in the sky. A... has not come back. The drawer of the chest to the left of the bed is still half open. Since it is quite heavy, it creaks as it slips back into place.

The bedroom door, on the contrary, turns silently on its hinges. The rubber-soled shoes make no sound on the hallway tiles.

To the left of the door to the veranda, the boy has arranged as usual the small table and single chair and the single cup of coffee on the table. The boy himself appears at the corner of the house, carrying in both hands the tray with the coffee pot on it.

Having set down his burden near the cup, he says: "Missy, she has not come back."

In the same tone he might have said, "The coffee, it is served", "God bless you" or anything at all. His voice invariably chants the same notes, so that it is impossible to distinguish questions from other sentences. Besides, like all the native servants, this boy is accustomed never to expect an answer to his questions. He immediately leaves again, this time going into the house through the open hall door.

The morning sun rakes this central part of the veranda, as it does the whole valley. In the almost cool air that follows daybreak, the singing of the birds has replaced that of the nocturnal crickets, and resembles it, though less even, embellished occasionally by a few somewhat more musical sounds. As for the birds, they are no more evident than the crickets – no more than usual – fluttering in concealment beneath the green clusters of the banana trees, all around the house.

In the zone of bare earth that separates the trees from the house, the ground sparkles with innumerable dew-covered webs, which the tiny spiders have spun beneath the clumps of dirt. Further down, on the log bridge over the little stream, a crew of five workmen is preparing to replace the logs which the termites have eaten away inside.

On the veranda, at the corner of the house, the boy appears, following his usual route. Six steps behind him comes a second black man, barefoot and wearing shorts and an undershirt, his head covered with an old, soft hat.

The gait of this second native is supple, lively and yet unconcerned. He advances behind his guide towards the coffee table without taking off his extraordinary shapeless, faded felt hat. He stops when the boy stops – that is, five steps behind him, and remains standing there, his arms hanging at his sides.

"The other master, he has not come back," the boy says.

The messenger in the soft hat looks up towards the beams, under the roof, where the pinkish-grey lizards chase each other in short, quick runs, suddenly stopping in the middle of their trajectory, heads raised and cocked to one side, tails frozen in the middle of an interrupted undulation.

"The lady, she is angry," the boy says.

He uses this adjective to describe any kind of uncertainty, sadness or disturbance. Probably he means "anxious" today, but it could just as well be "outraged", "jealous" or even "desperate". Besides, he has asked no questions; he is about to leave. Yet an ordinary sentence without any precise meaning releases from him a flood of words in his own language, which abounds in vowels, particularly As and Es.

He and the messenger are now facing each other. The latter listens, without showing the least sign of comprehension. The boy talks at top speed, as if his text had no punctuation, but in the same sing-song tone as when he is not speaking his own language. Suddenly he stops. The other does not add a word, turns around, and leaves by the same route he came in, with his swift, soft gait, swaying his head and hat, and hips, and arms beside his body, without having opened his mouth.

After having set the used cup on the tray beside the coffee pot, the boy takes the tray away, entering the house by the open door into the hallway. The bedroom windows are closed. At this hour A... is not up yet.

She left very early this morning, in order to have enough time to do her shopping and be able to get back to the plantation the same night. She went to the port with Franck, to make some necessary purchase. She has not said what they were.

Once the bedroom is empty, there is no reason not to open the blinds, which fill all three windows instead of glass panes. The three windows are similar, each divided into four equal rectangles – that is, four series of slats, each window frame comprising two sets hung one on top of another. The twelve series are identical: sixteen slats of wood, manipulated by a cord attached at the side to the outer frame.

The sixteen slats of a series are continually parallel. When the series is closed, they are pressed one against the other at the edge, overlapping by about half an inch. By pulling the cord down the pitch of the slats is reduced, thus creating a series of openings, whose width progressively increases.

When the blinds are open to the maximum, the slats are almost horizontal and show their edges. Then the opposite slope of the valley appears in successive, superimposed strips separated by slightly narrower strips. In the opening, at eye level, appears a clump of trees with motionless foliage at the edge of the plantation, where the yellowish brush begins. Many trunks are growing in a single cluster, from which the oval fronds of dark-green leaves branch out, so distinct they seem drawn one by one, despite their relative smallness and their great number. On the ground the converging trunks form a single stalk of colossal diameter, with projecting ribs that flare out as they near the ground.

The light quickly fades. The sun has disappeared behind the rocky spur that borders the main section of the plateau. It is six thirty. The deafening racket of the crickets fills the whole valley – a constant grating with neither nuance nor progression. Behind, the whole house has been empty since daybreak.

A… is not coming home for dinner, which she is taking in town with Franck before starting back. They will be home by about midnight, probably.

The veranda is empty too. None of the armchairs has been carried outside this morning, nor the table used for cocktails and coffee. Eight shiny points mark the place where the two chairs were set on the flagstones under the first window of the office.

Seen from outside, the open blinds show the unpainted edge of their parallel slats, where tiny scales are half detached here and there, which a fingernail could chip off without difficulty. Inside, in the bedroom, A... is standing in front of the window and looking through one of the chinks towards the veranda, the openwork balustrade and the banana trees on the opposite hillside.

Between the remaining grey paint, faded by time, and the wood greyed by the action of humidity, appear tiny areas of reddish brown – the natural colour of the wood – where the wood has been left exposed by the recent flaking off of new scales of paint. Inside her bedroom, A... is standing in front of the window and looking out between one of the chinks in the blinds.

The man is still motionless, leaning towards the muddy water, on the earth-covered log bridge. He has not moved an inch: crouching, head down, forearms resting on his thighs, hands hanging between his knees. He seems to be looking at something at the bottom of the little stream – an animal, a reflection, a lost object.

In front of him, in the patch along the other bank, several stems look ripe for cutting, although the harvest has not yet been started in this sector. The sound of a truck shifting gears on the highway on the other side of the house is answered here by the creak of a window lock. The first bedroom window is open.

The upper part of A...'s body is framed in it, as well as her waist and hips. She says "good morning" in the playful tone of someone who, having slept well, wakes up in a good mood – or of someone who prefers not to show what she is thinking about, always flashing the same smile on principle.

She immediately steps back inside, to reappear a little further on a few seconds afterwards – perhaps ten seconds, but at a distance of at least two or three yards – in the next window opening, where the blinds have just been opened. Here she stays no longer, her head turned towards the column at the corner of the terrace that supports the overhang of the roof.

From her post of observation, she can see only the green stretch of banana trees, the edge of the plateau and, between the two, a strip of uncultivated brush, high yellow weeds with a few scattered trees.

On the column itself there is nothing to see except the peeling paint and, occasionally, at unforeseeable intervals and at various levels, a greyish-pink lizard, whose intermittent presence results from shifts of positions so sudden that no one could say where it comes from or where it is going when it is no longer visible.

A… has stepped back again. To find her, the eye must be placed in the axis of the first window: she is in front of the big chest, against the rear wall of the bedroom. She opens the top drawer and leans over the right-hand side of the chest, where she spends a long time looking for something she cannot find, searching with both hands, shifting packages and boxes and constantly coming back to the same point, unless she is merely rearranging her effects.

In her present position, between the big bed and the hall door, other sight lines can easily reach her from the veranda, passing through one or another of the three open window recesses.

From a point on the balustrade located two steps from the corner, an oblique sight line thus enters the bedroom through the second window and cuts diagonally across the foot of the bed to the chest. A..., who has straightened up, turns towards the light and immediately disappears behind the section of the wall that separates the two windows and conceals the back of the large wardrobe.

She appears an instant later behind the left frame of the first window, in front of the writing table. She opens the leather writing case and leans forwards; the top of her thighs presses against the table edge. Her body, wider at the hips, again makes it impossible to follow what her hands are doing, what they are holding, picking up or putting down.

A... appears from a three-quarter view, as before, although from the opposite side. She is still in her dressing gown, but her hair, though loose, has already been carefully brushed; it gleams in the sunlight when her head, turning, shifts the soft, heavy curls, whose black mass falls on the white silk of her shoulder, while the silhouette again steps back towards the rear of the room along the hallway wall.

The leather writing case, parallel with the long side of the table, is closed, as usual. Above the varnished wood surface, instead of the hair, there is nothing but the post-office calendar, where only the white boat stands out from the grey tint of the wall behind.

The room now looks as if it were empty. A... may have noiselessly opened the hall door and gone out, but it is more likely that she is still there, outside the field of vision, in the blank area between this door, the large wardrobe and the corner of the table, where a felt circle constitutes the last visible object. Besides the wardrobe, there is only one piece of furniture (an armchair) in this area. Still, the concealed exit by which it communicates with the hall, the living room, the courtyard and the highway multiplies to infinity her possibilities of escape.

The upper part of A...'s body appears in the window opening in receding perspective from the third window, overlooking the west gable end of the house. At a given moment she must have passed in front of the exposed foot of the bed before entering the second blank area between the dressing table and the bed.

She stays there, motionless, for some time as well. Her profile is distinctly outlined against the darker background. Her lips are very red; to say whether they have been made up or not would be difficult, since it is their natural colour in any case. Her eyes are wide open, resting on the green mass on the banana trees, which they slowly move across as they approach the corner column with the gradual turning of the head and neck.

On the bare earth of the garden, the column's shadow now makes an angle of forty-five degrees with the perforated shadow of the balustrade, the western side of the veranda and the gable end of the house. A... is no longer at the window. Neither this window nor either of the two others reveals her presence in the room. And there is no longer any reason to suppose her in any one of the blank areas rather than in any other. Two of them, moreover, present an easy egress: the first into the central hallway, the other into the bathroom, whose other door opens onto hallway, the courtyard, etc... The bedroom again looks as if it were empty.

To the left, at the end of this western side of the veranda, the black cook is peeling yams over a tin basin. He is kneeling, sitting back on his heels, the basin between his thighs. The shiny pointed blade of the knife detaches an endless narrow peel from the long yellow tuber which revolves in his hand with a regular motion.

At the same distance but in the opposite direction, Franck and A... are drinking cocktails, sitting back in their usual armchairs under the office window. "That feels good!" Franck is holding his glass in his right hand, which is reposing on the elbow rest of the chair. The three other arms are stretched out parallel on the parallel strips of leather, but the three hands are lying palms down against the elbow rests, where the leather curves over the ridge before coming to a point just below three large nail heads, which attach it to the red wood.

Two of the four hands are wearing, on the same finger, the same gold ring, wide and flat: the first on the left and the third – which is holding a cylindrical glass half-filled with a golden liquid – Franck's right hand. A...'s glass is beside her on the little table. They are talking desultorily of the trip to the port they plan to make together during the following week, she for various purchases, he to find out about the new truck he intends to buy.

They have already settled the time of departure as well as that of the return, calculated the approximate duration of the ride and estimated the time in which they must settle their affairs. All that remains is to decide which day will best suit them both. It is only natural that A... should want to take advantage of such an occasion, which will permit her to make the trip under acceptable conditions without bothering anyone. The only surprising thing, really, is that such an arrangement has not already been made in similar circumstances previously, one day or another.

Now the tapering fingers of the second hand circle the large shiny nail heads: the ball of the last joint of the index finger, the middle finger and the ring finger circle round and round the three smooth, bulging surfaces. The middle finger is stretched out vertically, following the direction of the triangular point of the leather; the index and ring fingers are half bent to reach the two upper nail heads. Soon, twenty inches to the left, the same three delicate fingers of the other hand begin the same exercise. The furthest to the left of these six fingers is the one wearing the ring.

"Then Christiane doesn't want to come with us? That's too bad…"

"No, she can't," Franck says, "because of the child."

"And of course it's much hotter on the coast."

"More humid, yes, that's right."

"Still, it would be a change for her. How is she feeling today?"

"It's always the same thing," Franck says.

The low voice of the second driver, who is singing a native lament of some kind, reaches the three armchairs grouped in the middle of the veranda. Although distant, this voice is perfectly recognizable. Coming around each gable end at the same time, it reaches the ears simultaneously from right to left.

"It's always the same thing," Franck says.

A… presses the point, full of solicitude: "In town, though, she could see a doctor."

Franck raises his left hand from the leather armrest, but without lifting his elbow off, and then lets it fall back, more slowly, to where it was.

"She's already seen enough doctors as it is. With all those drugs she takes, it's as if she…"

"Still, you have to try something."

"But she claims it's the climate!"

"You can talk all you want about the climate, but that doesn't mean a thing."

"The attacks of malaria."

"There's quinine…"

Then five or six remarks are exchanged about the respective doses of quinine necessary in the various tropical regions, according to the altitude, the latitude, the proximity of the sea, the presence of swamps, etc… Then Franck refers again to the disagreeable effects quinine produces on the heroine of the African novel A… is reading. Afterwards he makes an allusion – obscure for anyone who has not even leafed through the book – to the behaviour of the husband, guilty of negligence, at least in the opinion of the two readers. His sentence ends in "take apart" or "take a part" or "break apart", "break a heart", "heart of darkness", or something of the kind.

But Franck and A… are already far away. Now they are talking about a young white woman – is it the same one as before, or her rival, or some secondary character? – who gives herself to a native, perhaps to several. Franck seems to hold it against her:

"After all," he says, "sleeping with black men…"

A… turns towards him, raises her chin, and asks smilingly: "Well, why not?"

Franck smiles in his turn, but answers nothing, as if he is embarrassed by the tone their dialogue is taking before a third person. The movement of his mouth ends in a sort of grimace.

The driver's voice has shifted. It now comes only from the east side: it apparently emanates from the sheds, to the right of the main courtyard.

The singing is at moments so little like what is ordinarily called a song, a complaint, a refrain, that the western listener is justified in wondering if something quite different is involved. The sounds, despite apparent repetitions, do not seem related to any musical law. There is no tune, really, no melody, no rhythm. It is as if the man were content to utter unconnected fragments as an accompaniment to his work. According to the orders he has received this very morning, this work must have as its object the impregnation of the new logs with an insecticide solution, in order to safeguard them against the action of the termites before putting them in place.

"Always the same thing," Franck says.

"Mechanical troubles again?"

"This time it's the carburettor… The whole engine has to be replaced."

On the handrail of the balustrade, a lizard is perched in absolute immobility: head raised and cocked towards the house, body and tail forming a flattened S. The animal looks as if it were stuffed.

"That boy has a lovely voice," A… says, after a rather long silence.

Franck continues: "We'll be leaving early."

A… asks him to be specific, and Franck gives details, asking if it is too early for his passenger.

"Not at all," she says. "It'll be fun."

They sip their drinks.

"If all goes well," Franck says, "we could be in town by ten and have a good bit of time before lunch."

"Of course I'd prefer that too," A… answers, her face serious again.

"I won't have too much time all afternoon finishing up my visits to the sales agents and asking the advice of my regular garage man, Robin – you know, down at the waterfront. We'll start back right after dinner."

The details he furnishes as to his schedule for this day in town would be more natural if they were provided to satisfy an interlocutor's question, but no one has shown the slightest interest today in the purchase of his new truck. And expressing his thoughts aloud – very loud – he comes close to giving the programme of his movements and his interviews yard by yard, minute by minute, constantly emphasizing the necessity of his behaviour in each case. A..., on the other hand, makes only the smallest reference to her own errands, the total duration of which will be the same, however.

For lunch, Franck is here again, loquacious and affable. This time Christiane has not accompanied him. They had almost had an argument the day before about the cut of a dress.

After the customary exclamation as to the comfort of the armchair, Franck begins telling, with a great wealth of detail, a story about a car with engine trouble. It is the sedan he is referring to, and not the truck; since the sedan is still almost new, it does not often give its owner problems.

The latter should, at this moment, refer to an analogous incident which occurred in town during this trip with A..., an incident of no importance but which postponed their return to the plantation by a whole night. The comparison would be only normal. Franck refrains from making it.

A... has been looking at her neighbour with increased attention these last few seconds, as if she were expecting a remark he was on the point of making. But she says nothing either, and the remark is not made. Besides, they have never again referred to that day, that accident, that night – at least when they are not alone together.

Now Franck is recapitulating the list of parts to dismantle for the complete inspection of a carburettor. He performs this exhaustive inventory with a concern for exactitude which obliges him to mention a number of elements that are ordinarily understood without being referred to; he goes almost to the point of describing the removal of a screw turn by turn and, similarly afterwards, for the converse operation.

"You seem to be up on your mechanics today," A... says.

Franck suddenly stops talking; in the middle of this account he looks at the lips and the eyes on his right, upon which a calm smile, as though with no meaning behind it, seems to be fixed by a photographic exposure. His own mouth has remained half open, perhaps in the middle of a word.

"In theory, I mean," A... specifies, without abandoning her most amiable tone of voice.

Franck turns his eyes away towards the openwork balustrade, the last flakes of grey paint, the stuffed lizard, the motionless sky.

"I'm beginning to get used to it," he says, "with the truck. All engines are alike."

Which is obviously untrue. The engine of his big truck, in particular, offers few points in common with that of his American car.

"That's right," A... says, "like women."

But Franck seems not to have heard. He keeps his eyes fixed on the pinkish-grey lizard opposite him, whose soft skin, under the lower jaw, throbs faintly.

A... finishes her glass of golden soda, sets it down on the table empty, and begins again to caress the three bulging nail heads on each leg of her chair with the tips of her six fingers.

Upon her closed lips floats a half-smile of serenity, reverie or abstraction. Since it is immutable and of too accomplished a regularity, it may also be false, entirely made up, polite or even imaginary.

The lizard on the handrail is now in shadow; its colours have turned dark. The shadow cast by the roof coincides exactly with the outlines of the veranda: the sun is at its zenith.

Franck, who was passing by and stopped in, declares he doesn't want to stay any longer. He actually stands up and sets down on the coffee table the glass he has just emptied in one gulp. He stops before walking down the hallway that crosses the house; he turns back to wave goodbye to his hosts. The same grimace, but swifter now, passes over his lips again. He disappears inside the house.

A... has not left her chair. She remains leaning back, arms stretched out on the elbow rests, eyes looking up at the empty sky. Beside her, near the tray with the two bottles and the ice bucket, there lies the novel Franck has lent her, which she has been reading since the evening before – a novel whose action takes place in Africa.

On the handrail of the balustrade, the lizard has disappeared, leaving in its place a flake of grey paint which seems to have the same shape: a body lying in the direction of the grain of the wood, a tail twisted into two curves, four rather short legs, and the head cocked towards the house.

In the dining room, the boy has laid only two places on the square table: one opposite the open pantry door and the long sideboard, the other on the window side. It is here that A... sits, her back to the light. She eats little, as usual. During almost the entire meal, she sits without moving, very straight on her chair, her hands with their tapering fingers framing a plate as white as the cloth, her gaze fixed on the brownish remains of the squashed centipede, which stain the bare wall in front of her.

Her eyes are very large, brilliant, green in colour, fringed with long curving lashes. They always seem to be seen from straight on, even when the face is seen in profile. She keeps them as wide as possible in all circumstances, without ever blinking.

After lunch, she returns to her chair in the middle of the veranda, to the left of Franck's empty chair. She picks up her book, which the boy left on the table when he took away the tray: she looks for the place where her first reading was interrupted by Franck's arrival, somewhere in the first part of the story. But having found the page again, she lays the open book face down on her knees and remains where she is without doing anything, leaning back in the leather chair.

From the other side of the house comes the sound of a heavy truck heading down the highway towards the bottom of the valley, the plain and the port – where the white ship is moored alongside the pier.

The veranda is empty, the house too. The shadow cast by the roof coincides exactly with the outlines of the veranda: the sun is at its zenith. The house no longer casts the slightest black band over the freshly spaded earth of the garden. The trunks of the thin orange trees also show no shadows.

It is not the sound of the truck that can be heard, but that of a sedan coming down the first road from the highway, towards the house.

In the open left leaf of the first dining-room window, in the middle of the central pane of glass, the reflected image of the blue car has just stopped in the middle of the courtyard. A... and Franck get out of it together, he on one side, she on the other, by the two front doors. A... is holding a tiny package of indeterminate shape, which immediately vanishes, absorbed by a flaw in the glass.

The two people immediately come closer together in front of the hood of the car. Franck's silhouette, larger than A...'s, conceals hers behind his. Franck's head is bent forwards.

The irregularities of the glass obscure the details of their actions. The living-room windows would give a direct view of the same spectacle and from a more convenient angle: both people seen side by side.

But they have already separated, walking side by side towards the door of the house, across the gravel of the courtyard. The distance between them is at least a yard. Under the precise noonday sun, they cast no shadows.

They are smiling at the same time – the same smile – when the door opens. Yes, they are in good health. No, there was no accident, only a little difficulty with the car which obliged them to spend the night at the hotel, waiting for a garage to open in the morning.

After a quick drink, Franck, who is in a great hurry to get back to his wife, stands up and leaves. His steps echo down the hallway tiles.

A... immediately goes to her bedroom, takes a bath, changes her dress, eats lunch with a good appetite, and returns to the veranda, where she sits down under the office window, whose blinds, three-quarters lowered, permit only the tip of her hair to be seen.

The evening finds her in the same position, in the same chair, in front of the same grey stone lizard. The only difference is that the boy has added the fourth chair, the one that is less comfortable, made of canvas stretched over a metal frame. The sun is hidden behind the rocky spur which comprises the western boundary of the chief section of the plateau.

The light rapidly fades. A..., who can no longer see clearly enough to continue reading, closes her novel and puts it down on the little table beside her (between the two groups of chairs: the pair with their backs against the wall beneath the window, and the two other dissimilar chairs placed at an angle nearer the balustrade). To mark her place, the outer edge of the shiny paper jacket protecting the cover has been inserted in the book, approximately a quarter of the way into it.

A... asks for today's news on the plantation. There is no news. There are only the trivial incidents of the cultivation work which periodically recur in one patch or another, according to the cycle of operations. Since the patches are numerous, and the plantation managed so as to stagger the harvest through all twelve months of the year, all the elements of the cycle occur at the same time every day, and the periodical trivial incidents also repeat themselves simultaneously, here or there, daily.

A... hums a dance tune whose words remain unintelligible. It may be a popular song she has heard in town, to the rhythm of which she may have danced once.

The fourth chair was superfluous. It remains vacant all evening long, further isolating the third leather chair from the other two. Franck, as a matter of fact, has come alone. Christiane did not want to leave the child, who has a little fever. It is not unusual nowadays that her husband comes without her for dinner. Tonight though,

A... seemed to expect her; at least she has had four places set. She orders the one which is not to be used to be taken away at once.

Although it is quite dark now, she orders the boy not to bring out the lamps, which – she says – attract mosquitoes. In the complete darkness, only the paler spots formed by a dress, a white shirt, a hand, two hands, soon four hands (the eyes getting used to the darkness) can be even guessed at.

No one speaks. Nothing moves. The four hands are lined up parallel to the wall of the house. On the other side of the balustrade, towards the hillside, there is only the starless sky and the deafening racket of the crickets.

During dinner, Franck and A... make a plan to go down to the port together some day soon, for various reasons. Their conversation returns to this projected trip after the meal, while they are drinking their coffee on the veranda.

When the violent cry of a nocturnal animal indicates its proximity – in the garden itself, at the south-west corner of the house – Franck suddenly stands up and walks with long strides to this side of the veranda; his rubber soles make no noise on the flagstones. In a few seconds his white shirt has completely vanished into the darkness.

Since Franck says nothing and does not return, A..., doubtless supposing he sees something, also stands up, supple and silent, and moves away in the same direction. Her dress is swallowed up in its turn by the opaque darkness.

After quite a long time, no word has yet been spoken loud enough to be heard at a distance of ten yards. It is also possible that there is no longer anyone in that direction.

Franck has left now. A... has gone into her bedroom. The interior of this room is lit, but the blinds are entirely closed: between the slats filter only a few tiny lines of light.

The violent cry of an animal, shrill and short, echoes again in the garden below, at the foot of the veranda. But this time it is from the opposite corner, facing the bedroom, that the signal seems to come.

. It is, of course, impossible to see anything, even leaning as far out as possible, the body halfway over the balustrade, against the square column, the column which supports the south-west corner of the roof.

Now the shadow of the column falls across the flagstones over this central part of the veranda in front of the bedroom. The oblique direction of the dark line points, when it is extended to the wall itself, to the reddish streak which has run down the vertical wall from the right corner of the first window, the one nearest the hallway.

The shadow of the column, though it is already very long, would have to be nearly a yard longer to reach the little round spot on the flagstones. From the latter runs a thin vertical thread which increases in size as it rises from the concrete substructure. It then climbs up the wooden surface, from lath to lath, growing gradually larger until it reaches the window sill. But its progression is not constant: the imbricated arrangement of the boards intercepts its route by a series of equidistant projections where the liquid spreads out more widely before continuing its ascent. On the sill itself, the paint has largely flaked off after the streak occurred, eliminating about three quarters of the red trace.

The spot has always been there on the wall. For the moment there is no question of repainting anything but the blinds and the balustrade – the latter a bright yellow. That is what A... has decided...

She is in her bedroom, whose two southern windows have been opened. The sun, very low in the sky now, is already much less warm, and when it strikes the façade directly, before disappearing, it will be only for a few seconds, at a raked angle, its beams entirely without strength.

A… is standing motionless in front of the writing table; she is facing the wall; she therefore appears in profile in the open window recess. She is rereading the letter received in the last post from Europe. The opened envelope forms a white rhombus on the varnished table top, near the leather writing case and the gold-capped fountain pen. The sheet of paper which she holds spread out in both hands still shows the creases where it has been folded.

Having read to the bottom of the page, A… puts the letter beside its envelope, sits down in the chair and opens the writing case. Out of the pocket of this, she takes a leaf of the same size, but blank, which she puts on the green blotter provided for this purpose. She then takes the cap off the pen and bends forwards to begin writing.

The shiny black curls tremble on her shoulders as the pen advances. Although neither the arm nor the head seems disturbed by the slightest movement, the hair, more sensitive, captures the oscillations of the wrist, amplifies them and translates them into unexpected eddies which awaken reddish highlights in its moving mass.

These propagations and interferences continue to multiply their interactions when the hand has stopped. But the head rises and begins to turn, slowly and steadily, towards the open window. The large eyes unblinkingly endure this transition to the direct light of the veranda.

Down below, in the hollow of the valley, in front of the patch shaped like a trapezoid, where the slanting rays of the sun outline each frond of the banana trees with extreme distinctness, the water of the little stream shows a ruffled surface which gives evidence of the swiftness of the current. It takes this last sunlight to reveal so clearly the successive chevrons and criss-crossings which the many interwoven ripples create. The wave moves on, but the surface remains as if petrified beneath these immutable lines.

Its brilliance is similarly fixed, and gives the liquid surface a more transparent quality. But there is no one to judge this on the spot – from the bridge, for instance. In fact, no one is in sight anywhere near. No crew is at work in this sector for the moment. Besides, the workday is over.

On the veranda, the shadow of the column is still longer. It has turned. It has almost reached the door to the house now, which marks the middle of the façade. The door is open. The hallway tiles are covered with chevron-shaped grooves, like those of the stream, though more regular.

The hallway leads straight towards the other door, the one that opens onto the entrance courtyard. The big blue car is parked in the middle. The passenger gets out and heads at once towards the house, without being inconvenienced by the gravel, despite her high-heeled shoes. She has been visiting Christiane, and Franck has brought her back.

The latter is sitting in his armchair, beneath the first office window. The shadow of the column moves towards him; after having diagonally crossed more than half the veranda, moved along the bedroom for its entire length, and passed the hallway door, it now reaches to the coffee table where A... has just put down her book. Franck is staying only a minute before going home; his workday is over too.

It is almost time for cocktails, and A... has not waited any longer to call the boy, who appears at the corner of the house, carrying the tray with the two bottles, three large glasses and the ice bucket. The route he follows over the flagstones is apparently parallel to the wall and converges with the line of shadow when he reaches the low, round coffee table where he carefully puts down the tray, near the novel with the shiny paper jacket.

It is the latter which provides the subject for the conversation. Psychological complications aside, it is a standard narrative of colonial life in Africa, with a description of a tornado, a native revolt and incidents at the club. A... and Franck discuss it animatedly, while sipping the mixture of cognac and soda served by the mistress of the house in the three glasses.

The main character of the book is a customs official. This character is not an official but a high-ranking employee of an old commercial company. This company's business is going badly, rapidly turning shady. This company's business is going extremely well. The chief character – one learns – is dishonest. He is honest, he is trying to re-establish a situation compromised by his predecessor, who died in an automobile accident. But he had no predecessor, for the company was only recently formed – and it was not an accident. Besides, it happens to be a ship (a big white ship) and not a car at all.

Franck, at this point, begins to tell an anecdote about a truck of his with engine trouble. A..., as politeness demands, asks for details to prove the attention she is paying to her guest, who soon stands up and takes his leave, in order to return to his own plantation, a little further east.

A... is leaning on the balustrade. On the other side of the valley, the sun rakes the isolated trees scattered over the brush above the cultivated zone. Their long shadows stripe the terrain with heavy parallel lines.

The stream in the hollow of the valley has grown dark. Already the northern slope receives no more light. The sun is hidden behind the rocky spur to the west. Outlined against the light, the silhouette of the rock wall appears distinctly for an instant against a violently illuminated sky: a sudden, barely swelling line which connects with the plateau by a sharp-pointed outcropping, followed by a less emphatic second projection.

Very quickly the luminous background becomes more sombre. On the opposite hillside, the clumps of banana trees grow blurred in the twilight.

It is six thirty.

Now the dark night and the deafening racket of the crickets again engulf the garden and the veranda, all around the house.

CALDER PUBLICATIONS

<small>SINCE 1949, JOHN CALDER</small> has published eighteen Nobel Prize winners and around fifteen hundred books. He has put into print many of the major French and European writers, almost single-handedly introducing modern literature into the English language. His commitment to literary excellence has influenced two generations of authors, readers, booksellers and publishers. We are delighted to keep John Calder's legacy alive and hope to honour his achievements by continuing his tradition of excellence into a new century.

❧

<small>ANTONIN ARTAUD:</small> *The Theatre and Its Double*

<small>LOUIS-FERDINAND CÉLINE:</small> *Journey to the End of the Night*

<small>MARGUERITE DURAS:</small> *The Sailor from Gibraltar*

<small>ERICH FRIED:</small> *100 Poems without a Country*

<small>EUGÈNE IONESCO:</small> *Plays*

<small>LUIGI PIRANDELLO:</small> *Collected Plays*

<small>RAYMOND QUENEAU:</small> *Exercises in Style*

<small>ALAIN ROBBE-GRILLET:</small> *In the Labyrinth*

<small>ALEXANDER TROCCHI:</small> *Cain's Book*

To order any of our titles and for up-to-date information about our current and forthcoming publications, please visit our website on:

www.almaclassics.com